I0817955

DO NOT MISS ALAN DALE DICKINSON'S

PREVIOUSLY PUBLISHED CRIME-FICTION MYSTERIES:

Charlie O'Brien, Private Investigator

Kidnap Country

The Money Changer

For the Love of Money

Charlie's Private Eye Angels

Orange County (California) Confidential

Baghdad Confidential

A Mystery in Laguna Woods

A Theft in Laguna Woods

A Kidnapping in Laguna Woods

A Shooting in Laguna Woods

In addition, a published short primer on:

How to Write (and publish) a Novel

The City of Brotherly Love

A CHARLIE O'BRIEN PRIVATE INVESTIGATOR MYSTERY

The City of Brotherly Love

A CHARLIE O'BRIEN PRIVATE INVESTIGATOR MYSTERY

BY PROFESSOR
ALAN DALE DICKINSON

ISBN: 978-1-7326283-3-5

DICKINSON PUBLISHING COMPANY
PROFESSOR ALAN DALEDICKINSON
Chairman and Chief Executive Officer

Bank of America
Vice President and Business Banking Manager (Retired)
World Corporate Lending Group
P.O. Box 3962
Laguna Hills, CA 9265

DEDICATION

To Howard B. Crawford, Jan Smoker, OCSD *Sergeant J. J. Hernandez,* Leann Anderson, John Anderson, Lindsay Anderson, Zach Anderson, Dr. Anne E. Ford, Dr. Brett Long and Bailey, Karin Carpenter, Natalie Holm, Riverside County Sheriff Chad Bianco, OCSD Sheriff Don Barnes, OCSD Undersheriff Robert Peterson, and OCSD Special Community Citizen Assistance Program and Department, *Captain Jason Danks.*

And, OC District Attorney, Todd Spitzer, California *Attorney General Xavier Becerra*, AG, Mark Alan Dickinson, Captain David Alan Dickinson, (one of the bravest police officers in the OC), and Chief of Police, John Burks, both of the Brea PD. Chief Burks is an outstanding career law enforcement professional who has spent most of his illustrious career at the Brea Police Department. And OCSD Sergeant, *Kevin Lybrand,* the new kid on the block, but a very sharp and 'street' smart officer.

My dear friends, Peggy Edwards, Miranda McPhee, Natalie Holm, Jennifer Karmarkar, a terrific Free Speech Editor, Alma, and long time and great personal friends, Thomas and Pamela Rose, Don (a master story teller), and god friend.

Danny and Hope, Peter and Grace, Jim and Betty, Kris and Sudka and Mehta, Jo Nell, Carol and Cliff, and Ken and Jo, also, Angie, and Adara. Dennis and Denise.

Also, Sue, Sandy, four Judies, my good friend, Ray, Irene, Diane wonderful greeting card maker, Otella, Janet, and a new friend (Amigo) Richie Sanchez, Ollie, Pat, Marilou, Tim, and Patrick, a very talented, musical wizard.

Sister, Jan and John Stolba, cat lovers like Charlie, and sister Lisa and Bob Pike, rescue dog lovers. Deanna Estes, my great editor, Desiree' and Morgan Dickinson.

In addition, to all of the dedicated law enforcement officers, the good women and men deputies and police officers in the OC (Orange County) and Riverside County, California. These brave and fearless individuals risk their 'life and limbs' on a daily basis, to protect the women, children, and less fortunate people in this area.

SPECIAL DEDICATION

To Lovely Lynn, who is my Sun, my Moon and my Stars. And also, my inspiration for writing and my reason for living.

CHAPTER ONE

THERE HAS BEEN another 'smash and grab' at a local high-end jewelry store, also another bank robbery at the 'Bank of America' branch downtown Philly, as well as yet another drive-by shooting in the 'hood' (the 75th this year, alone).

All of these tragic events occurred on the east side of Philly (*Philadelphia*, Pennsylvania). The Police Commissioner, Chief and Coroner, Leann Anderson, called our man Charles 'Charlie' Werner Kennedy O'Brien, the famous and or infamous, depending upon who you ask, Private Investigator out in La-La Land (Los Angeles, California) for help.

Commissioner Anderson, whose husband, Big John and smart and hardworking daughter, Lindsay, are both attorneys', and whose son, Zach, is a successful business executive. And John was a former assistant District Attorney and handled dangerous prosecutions in southern California against 'gang bangers' and 'crooked' politicians.

John was a brilliant litigator and outstanding in presenting his cases to the Jury. Lindsay, was very intelligent as well as quite creative and just loves 'Armadillos'. Charlie told people when Lindsay was a little kid, back in the day, that he knew, just knew for certain that when she grew up, she would be an extremely bright, successful, and a very good person. He truly did. And as usual, he was right, she is!

Chief Anderson, asked Charlie to set up a 'Task Force' to assist the local Philly PD (Police Department) solve this very frightening City Crime Wave. The whole city was up-in-arms and worried sick about all of the continued violence and mayhem!

The Chief, who was once a paralegal, raised her two absolutely wonderful kids, then got her Law Degree, went on to become a Police Detective with the OCSD (Orange County Sheriff's Department) in California, and just recently moved and became the first woman ever Philly Police Commissioner in 'The City of Brotherly Love.'

She is a 2020's kind of woman; intelligent, brave, hardworking, and lets nothing stand in her way to 'serve and protect' the women, children and less fortunate people, in *California* and now in Philadelphia. Chief Anderson, even sings in her Church choir in Philly on weekends and has a voice like an 'angel' according to Charlie.

As soon as Charlie hung up his encrypted-satellite cell phone, he immediately called, *Howard Crawford*, ex-CIA Director, *Jan*

Smoker, ex-CIA Assistant Director, and his loyal and very good personal friend, Sarge.

Sarge, was *Sergeant J. J. Hernandez*, of the OCSD (Orange County Sheriff Department-Special Operations Unit), Santa Ana, California. Luckily for Charlie, he was on a one- year leave of absence, from the OCSD.

He had been wounded, pretty badly actually, in a "Shooting in Laguna Woods," California, a few months ago. He had been assisting Charlie in solving several shootings in that lovely community, which is just east of the beautiful seaside village of Laguna Beach. People travel from all over the world to visit Laguna Beach.

The Orange County Sheriff, Don Barnes, and also the Orange County District Attorney, Todd Spitzer, said that Charlie could borrow the Sarge' for a few weeks to assist him with his investigation in Philly, but that he needed to bring the Sarge "back all 'in one-piece."

Charlie had also requested, at the same time, that OCSD Sergeant *Kevin Lybrand* come along with Sarge just to help out. Sort of a 'package' deal. Kevin was the new kid on the block at the *Community* Policing department of the Sheriff's department.

He was very 'street' smart, well-educated by the OCSD, quick to laugh just like his cool coworker, and also like Sarge, not afraid of anything nor anybody. He worked patrol, and the 'jails' for several years prior to this current promotion.

Charlie had responded to them both, "Thanks a lot, I really need him to 'watch my back' but do not tell him I said that or he will get a big head, and his head is already too big." Then he laughed, and they both laughed with him, they all laughed a lot.

Charlie had worked on several criminal investigations with both the 'New Sheriff' in Town, and also the OCDA. Also, Chief Anderson and her husband, John, had worked with the two of them in the OC (Orange County) previously as well.

Chief Anderson told Chief Barnes on her encrypted satellite cell phone, "Charlie and Sarge remind me of *Laurel and Hardy*, or *Bud Abbott and Lou Costello,* what about you?"

Chief Barnes laughed, then laughed again, and even laughed a third time, "No Chief Anderson, they remind me of '*Rowan and Martin'* from the hit TV show "Laugh-In."

Then the OCDA, Todd Spitzer, said (it was a three -way conference phone call), "No you are both wrong, they remind me of *'Tom and Dicky' Smothers* from the very funny 'Smothers Brothers' comedy TV show."

When Sarge heard about the phone call, and how funny all three of the Chief's thought it was, thought it was funny them 'trash talking' them, Sarge told Charlie, "Do you know what they are calling us, Senior?"

Charlie said, "I can only imagine, laughed and then said, but go ahead and tell me, poncho." After Sarge told Charlie about all of the comparisons from the phone call, Charlie said, "All three of them are wrong, completely wrong, we are more like 'Sonny *Crockett* and Ricardo *Tubbs'*, from the outstanding '*Miami Vice'* TV police detective show from the 1980's."

Charlie told Sarge that he used to watch it every week with his two sons when they were just kids, now, their, both career cops now themselves. Charlie just loved the sound-track by the great rock n' roll singer, Phil Collins (of Genesis). And his theme song for the show, 'In the Air Tonight'.

Sarge spoke up loudly and then said, "I want to be *Sonny* this time, you got to be him when we were at the 'Shooting in Laguna Woods Village'. And you can be Tubbs this time around."

Charlie, said emphatically, "Sarge I make a better Crockett than you do, and you make a better Ricardo Tubbs than I do, know what I mean?" Sarge rebuffed, "No, old man I do not agree with you and also it is only fair that we change rolls on each criminal investigation, don't you agree boss?"

"OK, ok, alright, enough you, big cry baby, Sarge, you can be 'Sonny Crockett' and I will be 'Ricardo Tubbs', But, *only* this one time and *next* time I go back to being Sonny because he is one of my heroes and alter-ego."

Sarge got a great big smile all over his face, slapped old Charlie on the back, and said, "Thanks a lot Jefa, you're a real sport, you really are." Then he added, "And, yes you can be your hero Sonny next time, no problem."

Chad Bianco, Sheriff RCSD (Riverside County Sheriff Department) was Chief Andersons next important encrypted phone call. Sheriff Bianco, Chief Anderson and her husband John, as well as Charlie went way back.

Riverside, California is right next to the OC (Orange County) and the OCSD and the RCSD work together quite often to serve and protect both very large communities.

Sarge also knew Sheriff Bianco and later on he told Charlie that Sheriff was the 'real deal', he was known, even in his Sheriff position, to be the first through the door when apprehending a wanted felon.

He had worked all over Riverside County before being elected, by a landslide, to be the RCSD Sheriff. All the way to Los Angeles County, San Bernardino County, the OC, and San Diego.

Sheriff Bianco graduated from the RCSD Training Academy at the top of his class. He was an expert marksman, had a black -

belt in 'Tae kwon do' and Karate and also taught hand to hand combat for new recruits at the Academy.

Chief Anderson asked Sheriff Bianco if she could borrow his 'undersheriff' to assist in these heinous and vicarious criminal activities in 'The City of Brotherly Love?" She then added it should only take about three months max since she had Charlie, Jan and Sarge already on their way.

He immediately said, "No problem Leann, and how is big John doing, and by the way how do you like the cold freezing winters and hot and humid summers in Philly?" Then he laughed and laughed some more. The Sheriff, just like Charlie and Leann, has a terrific sense of humor.

^^^^^

Before Charlie got on the jet-plane for Philly, he called his outstanding Chiropractor, Brett Long, DC and asked him if her could meet him in Philadelphia because he was going to need him.

His back, neck and feet were bothering him, badly. Also, several of his former GSW's (gun-shot wounds) were acting up again. Doctor Long was the best chiropractor in all of Orange County, and also the whole State of California, in our man Charlie's opinion.

Doctor Long's lovely fiancé, name of Bailey, was a part time Private Investigator (private detective) in the OC (Orange County, California). She was as intelligent as she was attractive, quick, street smart, and very resourceful. Also, she could find anybody anywhere no matter how hard they tried to hide from the authorities.

Charlie told the doc and Bailey, that he would pay all of the expenses, regular class of course, only he gets to travel first class. Sarge on the Q.T. told the Doc and Bailey that "Charlie is a spoiled brat sometimes."

Secret, Doc Long loves, just loves donuts, all shapes and sizes, but Bailey won't let him eat them because she told him, "She did not want him to get fat like old Charlie."

She was just kidding, of course. The doc is like a son to our man Charlie, he has helped him 'keep on going' even when he was severely injured, healed his several battle wounds, as well as a TBI (Traumatic Brian Injury) with a fractured skull and 'severe' concussion last year while he was playing tennis.

Charlie not only wanted the Doc to come to Philly, to help with his old 'war' wounds, but also to be close just in case he got shot and or stabbed, Again. He told Sarge once, "I cannot tell you how many times that I have been hurt and injured 'on the job."

Then Sarge spit back, "Jefa, are you bragging or complaining?" To which Charlie retorted, "Both, and you are just jealous my Latino niño, because you have only been nicked before in the line of duty."

Also, Charlie needed Bailey, to come along because he wanted her to assist him in trying to find our who was committing the 'crime wave' in Philly. She knew how to 'work the streets' and CI's (confidential informants) as well as the internet to find some viable suspects for him, Jan, Howard, and Sarge to zero in on. She could save him hours and weeks because she is so efficient at these challenges.

Charlie told Bailey, "That if I was 100 years younger and not married to an absolutely exquisite, intelligent and tall model wife, I would, flirt with you. He said this in front of Doc, of course, and then laughed, and laughed some more.

The Doc responded to Charlie, "I understand completely, you have good taste, she is just a fantastic catch, believe me I know, and except for your quite lovey bride, and you being old enough to be her grandfather, you would be perfect for her." Then all three of them laughed, and laughed some more, with Charlie laughing the loudest, naturally.

The Doc and Bailey are two of Charlies BBF's (Best Friends forever). They truly are. Charlie Told Sarge that they were two of the nicest and brightest people he as met in years.

He loved them both, very dearly and would do anything, anything at all for them, if they needed him. Charlie knows lots and lots of people, all over the Globe actually, however, Doc and Bailey are two of the nicest people he has ever met, ever.

Charlie can call either 24/7 if he is in a bad state or has been injured (again). Some people in your life make it better, and others make it a lot worse. The Doc and Bailey make Charlie's life better, a lot better.

Charlie had to make just one more encrypted satellite cell phone call, before he got into his first -class seat with the pretty flight attendants. He never flirts with them because his lovely bride is better looking that they are and also, she has the longest and the best legs in the nation.

They always flirt with old Charlie, anyway and when he tells Sarge about them, he replies, "Yes, Charlie my egoistic friend, I am sure, but you ever notice that the pretty and efficient flight attendants that flirt with you forgot their eye contacts or glasses?"

Charlie, "What? Did you say Sarge?" Sarge, "I do not mean to burst your bubble my senior citizen boss, but when you look in the mirror and see a 6'4" tall, dark and handsome dashing PI, that the rest of the world sees, it makes you jealous."

Charlie to Sarge, "Thanks, Sarge I needed that, not, and remind me on my next criminal investigation, to leave you behind in the OC at the OCSD."

He called '*Karin Carpenter*'. She has the same name as the absolutely *marvelous* singer of the 'Carpenter's', back in the day (however it is pronounced Kar-in). That was 'Karen' Carpenter though, and Charlie really loved her angelic, voice, and he cried like a baby when she died, way, way to young!

Karin was a good friend and she was an accomplished attorney as well as a Private Investigator. She had two terrific kids, well young adults actually, a son and a daughter. She liked mystery and suspense novels and thought that Charlie was a righteous dude.

And she was also a good friend of *Doctor Anne E. Ford*, Charlies private and personal on call -physician. Also, she was quite well educated, a wonderful listener, very thorough in her paperwork and court pleadings.

Charlie needed her help on several recent occasions and she was always there for him. Rain or shine. She really was. And Charlie told Sarge that Karin was coming to Philly to assist with the criminal investigation and that she would be a big asset to them.

When Charlie introduced Sarge to Karin, Sarge told Charlie, in private naturally, "Wow, Karin is really something. She is intelligent, charming, dresses impeccably, a wonderful mom, and looks like she is about 30 years old."

And then continued, "Also, she has quite lovely long blonde hair. And you know Charlie how I love long hair. And she is interested in other people instead of herself like some beautiful women."

Finally, Charlie cut Sarge off and said, "Alright my son, I hear you loud and clear, and I totally agree with you, but how about we focus on the 'crime wave' instead of how attractive, and smart Karin is?"

Sarge to Charlie, "Ok, alright, you party pooper, I was just saying."

Then Sarge says to Charlie, "Hey old man, senior Charlie, do you think you are up to this latest investigation in 'The City of Brotherly Love?" Laughed as usual, the Sarge loves to laugh, he really does, has a great sense of humor Charlie always says, that is one of the reasons he always gets him to assist on his dangerous missions.

Sarge keeps things light for old Charlie, and also, and more importantly, much more importantly, is that Charlie knows that Sarge always has his back no matter how bad things get and also always has his *'head on a swivel'* watching out for the bad guys.

Sarge tilted his head, and ten tilted it a little bit more, and then said to Charlie, "Old man, my favorite all time Hefa, I know that you think that you know everything, but of course you do not. So, I want to teach you the Call (i.e. Ten) Codes for my great OCSD (Orange County California Sheriff's Department)."

He took a breath, and continued, "You worked for the LAPD (Los Angeles Police Department) so you know the 'wrong' 10 codes. You think that A stands for Adam, but it does not, A stands for Alpha." And more, "And here are the rest of the correct 10 codes my senior citizen."

10-1. Receiving poorly.

10-2. Receiving well.

10-3. Stop transmitting.

10-4. Acknowledged.

10-5. Relay.

10-6. Busy.

10-7. Out of service.

10-8. In service.

10-9. Repeat.

10-10. Out of vehicle.

10-11. Transmitting too fast.

10-12. Visitor present.

10-13. N/A.

10-14. Escort.

10-15. En-route with passenger.

10-16. Pick up passenger.

10-17. Pick up package.

10-18. N/A.

10-19. Return to post.

10-20. Location.

10-21. Telephone call.

10-22. Cancel.

10-23. Standby.

10-24. to 10.32 N/A.

10-33. Emergency radio traffic.

10-34. Resume normal traffic.

10-35. Confidential Information.

10-36. Correct time.

10-37 to 10-38 N/A.

10-39. Message delivered.

10-40 to 10-10-47 N/A.

10-48. Ready.

10-49 to 10-65 N/A.

10-66. Suspicious activity.

10-67 to 10- 86 N/A.

10-87 Meet with representative.

10-88 to 10-90 N/A.

10-91. Investigate.

10-92 to 10-95 N/A.

10-96. En-route respond.

10-97. On scene.

10-98. Completed assignment.

10-99 Officer needs immediate assistance.

10-100. Restroom/lunch break.

Sarge to Charlie, "Now you see the correct Ten-codes to use when you use you police scanner/radio. You do not use the old LAPD codes, from now on you need to use the OCSD ten codes, got it Hefa?"

Charlie, to Sarge, "Si my little amigo, I will use your ten-codes from now but I want you to know that I still like my old LAPD codes better, But if it will help you keep your, mouth shut, even for a little while, I will gladly do so."

CHAPTER TWO

JUST AS SOON as Sarge, Jan and Charlie 'rolled' up to the Philly PD's (Police Department's) 10th Precinct, they started taking gun fire, a lot of gun fire. Chief Anderson had agreed to meet them at this particular Police sub-station because it was a ground zero for most of the heinous and vicarious recent criminal activity.

The rental car, that they had picked-up at the Philadelphia airports, an almost brand- new BMW 750 IL, with a 'V-8' engine, and all of the 'bells and whistles' and practically drove itself, was riddled with bullet holes. About 50 of them. And all of them seemed to come from AK-47's and Mac-10's, fully automatic weapons!

Charlie and Sarge could tell what type of guns were being used to burry them 6 feet under the old 'cobblestone' Philly street, by hearing them on many, many other occasions before.

By the way, Charlie and his A-Team ('crew' and/or 'posse' as he calls them) flew First Class from Los Angeles, California to Philadelphia. He always flies first class because he is a big man (he thinks anyway) and needs a big boy seat. Also, he likes all of the special attention he gets in first class and also the very friendly, attractive and helpful women flight attendants.

Sarge was shot in the right earlobe, and also in his right shoulder. Charlie was driving, he always drives, always. Sarge says that it is because, "Charlie is a control freak." Then Charlie always responds and states, "No I am not a control freak, I just like being in control." Yeah, right Charlie our man.

Jan was in the back seat, since the Airport. Charlie called her, "A back seat driver," and then laughed, he was always laughing at all of his own jokes because according to Sarge, "nobody else does." Poor Charlie, he tries.

She did not get shot by the dirty sniper due to her fast thinking, she fell on the floor behind the front seats and the rear seats and was away from the windows. Also, she covered her head with an umbrella she had in her purse.

You never know when it is going to rain in Philly, she told Charlie and Sarge, she had grown up in Philly and knew the climate there very well. There was lots of glass from the bullet holes in the windows, but the umbrella kept it off of her head and face. Quick thinking Jan, very quick thinking.

Charlie got clipped in the left forearm and left temple and his neck. He grimmest and moaned, but just a little bit, because

Sarge said, "Charlie you cry like a baby, that could not hurt that much and besides you did not hear me moan, did you?"

Charlie told Sarge, "Why don't you shut up, fougasse, and yes, I did hear you whimper a little bit just when you got hit." Then he added, "You rotten sucker, you are going to pay for shooting up my crew and myself, and you are going to pay sorely, you really are."

Sarge added in response, "No Charlie I did not whimper, at all, that was just your over active imagination, once again." And then continued, "But yes this sneaky and cowardly would be killer will pay for this ambush, and he shall pay soon, real soon."

Charlie, moaned again, even more loudly this time, and replied, "Sarge you are 100% correct, he and/or she, will receive 'street' justice, very, very, soon. I only wish I was up to doing it myself."

In less than a heartbeat, Chief Anderson and what appeared to Charlie to be about 100 of Philly PD's finest (PPD), were surrounding the bullet ridden and once quite lovely jet black, BMW.

Then they carried, very, very quickly, all three of the A-Team into the Police Precinct and at the same time other brave souls moved in tandem right into the 'lions' den and the spot where the AK-47's and the Mac-10's were 'barking' from.

While Chief Anderson and her senior officers were placing Sarge, Jan and old Charlie into the small but very well - equipped Police ER room, in the back of the Precinct, they had a doctor on call at all times.

The doctor, Dr. Martin King, MD, who it just so happed was at the sub-station putting away supplies just in case any of the good officers got shot and/or stabbed. He was an excellent GP (General Practitioner) who specialized in GSW's (Gun shot wounds).

He had a very large medical office downtown Philly and was busy 24/7. He had a quite large patient base and all of them thought that he was the best doctor in Philly, and perhaps the whole country.

The good Doctor immediately put each of Charlies crew on separate hospital gurneys and then went from one to the other taking care of the worst gsw's first. He also had to reset a few shattered bones, patching up gun- shot holes, as well as putting on tons of bandages.

Meanwhile 'back at the ranch', the large group of police officers outside the front door of the precinct, about 50 or so, surrounded the building from which the nasty bullets were fired.

Four officers were, unfortunately, wounded crossing the '*gauntlet*' (open area) between the Station and the building. Luckily, they were not seriously injured and their fellow officers rushed them back to the ER room at the precinct where Dr. King was working on Sarge, Jan and Charlie.

The rest of the officers grabbed their SWAT gear from their cars parked out front of the Station, and approached the 'perpetrators' office building and lair. They each had full body armor, helmets, knee pads, and gloves in their police cruisers.

Also, they each had a shot-gun, fully locked and loaded, which they grabbed as they hurriedly put on their gear. They already had their AR-15's at the ready and within a few moments, they were armed to the teeth and ready and willing to go!

He and/or she or they, were on the third floor of the old and run-down three-story office building. The perp, or perps, were firing from an open office window which looked right down on the front door to the Police Station.

From there they had a completely unobstructed view of the '*killing* field.' Charlie later told Sarge that it was like "shooting fish in a barrel." So, to speak.

What was not clear, at least not at that exact moment, was why, Charlie and his great A-team, were singled out and question number two, how did the shooter and or shooters, know that they were in Philly from LA?

And question number three was, how did the bad guys and or bad girls, know the exact time that Charlie and crew would be at that particular Police Precinct?

Besides knowing when and where they were going to be, somebody, also knew the exact day and time (2 p.m.=1400) that they would arrive?

Captain *Danks* was the first to reach the third floor, the elevator was broken, so he had to run all the way up three flights of stairs. Luckily, he was in good shape, as he worked -out in the Police gym every morning before his shift.

When he reached the front door to the office suite that the bullets were raining down from, he did not hesitate, he kicked the door wide open with his size 13 police issue boots, and the door splintered like a match box.

As soon as he was inside, he yelled, as loudly, as he possible could;" Philly PD, drop your weapons, and do it *now*."

The lone gunman dressed in all black with body armor all over, was still at the window shooting at the police in front of the Station.

He was holding a brand new and fully automatic AK-47 with 15 round bullet clips, two of them taped back to back, and strapped to his chest was the hated Mac-10 (a favorite with gang bangers in Philly and also all over the nation these days).

Also, he had a 45- caliber auto pistol hung on each of his legs just like in the movies, they were model 1911's, a very, very dangerous gun. And strapped to his back was a 15- inch K-Bar marine combat knife.

Then the gunman holding his AK-47 killing machine, immediately spun completely around facing Captain Danks, and without hesitation yelled, "I am gonna kill you pig, like I just killed that nosey PI from LA and his two sidekicks."

^^^^^

That was a mistake, a big mistake, criminals did not talk to the Captain like that, not if they were smart and wanted to live anyway. Just as the cold- blooded shooter aimed his AK at the door the Cap opened fire with his AR-15 police automatic rifle.

The assassin had in a split second, got off a few rounds from his AK-47 and he had hit three of the female police officers who were standing shoulder to shoulder with Captain Danks.

Fortunately, none of the three were hurt very badly, and they were moved down the stairs, immediately by their fellow officers who were standing just outside of the doorway.

One was hit in the foot right through her steel-toed police boot, another in the shoulder which was not covered by her body armor, and the third in her arm.

Sadly, the Cap was also hit by the flurry of AK gun fire. He was hit in the leg, but he did not even make a sound, tough guy, really tough.

The Killer immediately dropped his empty AK on the floor and grabbed for his Mac-10 tied to his chest, but before he could open fire with it against the police, Captain *Danks* and his brave and fearless officers stepped forward, and bent low.

Now, even though some of them had been wounded, they opened up with their AR-15's (fully automatic assault rifles), and blew the dirty rotten murderer right out of the third -story window at his back.

Almost immediately after they shot him 15 times, or so, they heard a loud smash, a very loud noise. The gunman had landed on the roof of a beautiful classic 1970 Ford Mustang (or Pony car, as Sarge called it).

The classic beauty was red and worth about $25,000.00 on the market. Charlie was sick when her heard, no not about the assassin being killed but about the car being ruined.

Charlie has had a life-long love affair and/or affection for Classic cars. He truly has, ever since he was about 13 years old and growing up in the La Puente/El Monte barrio. He loves Latino people to this very day, and considers himself to be part Mexican, as they called themselves back in the day, inside.

He always said how nice they were to him even though he was one of a few white kids in the hood. Even the gang bangers were his friends, they said he made them laugh.

They would beat up or stab the other white kids, but not Charlie. They had 'zip' guns back then and did not have the Mac's and AK's that the bangers have today. They called him hermanito pequeno or little kid brother.

Charlies Spanish (Espanola) is not very good, as you can plainly see, but he can swear in Spanish, just like a drunken sailor, when he loses his temper, naturally.

Back in the Police ER, Sarge looked over at Jan and said, "Are you alright little woman?" Jan laughed but it hurt, some, and then replied, "Who are you calling little?".

Then they both laughed. Right after that, Sarge yelled over at Charlie, who was on the other side of Jan, and said, "Another *fine mess* you got me into, Charlie. I think that it was *'Laurel and Hardy'* who used to say that back, in the 1940's.

Or maybe it was Bud *Abbott* and Lou *Costello*, anyway, Charlie remembered the reference and shot back to Sarge, "What are you complaining about, you got a free, first -class round trip plane ticket to the 'City of Brotherly Love' didn't you?"

"Charlie, you cry like a little baby every time you get a little owie." Charlie almost got up out of his hospital bed, but it hurt too bad, so he just retorted, “Sarge, remind me to leave you back in the OC (Orange Country, California) on my next investigation.”

“Fine why don’t you do that, old man mosses, but then who is going to watch your back, if I am not there? And also, I think you have forgotten about the time that I saved your ‘bacon’ back in Laguna Woods Village (Laguna Woods, California) right by the lovely ocean front City of Laguna Beach.

Charlie loved to tease Sarge and Sarge loved to tease our man Charlie. I think it was what kept them both alive and made life more fun and interesting. At least that is my humble opinion.

Chief Anderson came into the Police ER right after they ‘took’ down the assassin, and asked good Dr. King how her three patients (Jan, Sarge, and Charlie) and also her several officers who had been wounded, were doing.

The Doc told her everyone was fine, except for Charlie and he had a severe ego injury. He seems to think that he is infallible and should not have allowed himself to get shot?

The Chief was relieved that all of her peeps and Jan, Sarge and Charlie were alright and would be back on the job in no time, no time at all. Meanwhile out side the good Philly Trans people were cleaning up all of the mess, the broken glass from the windows, and towed away the beautiful classic Ford Pony.

Charlie sent a message to the owner, and told him that he would buy the *Mustang* from him for a fair amount ($13,000.00) and then he was going to repair it back to its original condition.

Charlie has a bunch of 'classic' cars in the huge garage behind his Beverly Hills mansion. His favorite was his 1964 *Chevy Impala* with a 409 big block V-8 engine, 4 speeds on the floor, and posi-traction in the back.

It was repainted in the original Beautiful Maroon color (cost $12,000.00) and black imported leather bucket seats (not original) in front and a recently added 15 speaker 'surround' sound music system.

People could hear our PI coming for miles, in the quiet and *toney* neighborhood when he 'cranked' up his tunes. He loves Motown (Barry Gordie, and Smokin' 'Smokey' Robinson), are the greatest record producers, of all times.

Charlie saw both of these legions at the Cerritos Performing Art Center (in Cerritos, California) recently, and The Chicago Blues (Robert Johnson, so great and soulful), and Classic Rock/Pop, of course (mostly from the 1980's).

'Fleetwood Mac', The Rolling Stones, and the Best band ever, the Beatles (Charlie saw Ringo Starr perform Live at the "Pechenga Hotel and Casino" in Temecula, California, a few years ago), and more! He says Sir Paul McCartney was his favorite Beatle, however, he loved them all.

Sarge always tells him, "No, old man, John Lennon was the best Beatle, he was the heart and soul of the band, not Sir Paul." To which Charlie always retorts, "You are just a kid Sarge, and you did not even see them Live on the *"Ed Sullivan Show"* back in the day, like I did, so you do not know any better."

Our man Charlie, just loves this car, a lot, and Sarge asked him one day, "Charlie, old man, you seem to be obsessed with your '64 Impala, why is that Jefa?" Then Charlie replied, "Nino, my good friend in high school had one just like that and we used to go 'cruising' Pasadena.

And also *'made* the scene in, El Monte, La Puente, West Covina and Whittier (Southern California) in that car, all of the time. Good times *and* good memories, that is why, my little nosey son."

The next day Chief Anderson called Charlie at his hotel [Hilton Hotel at Penn's Landing] and told him that they had identified the filthy and cowardly sniper. His name was 'Abdul Mohamed al-Yemini'.

The very lovely, and quite famous *Hilton Hotel* was located right on the historical *Delaware River* on the very popular *Penn's Landing* (Harbor). Charlie got the 'penthouse' suite on the top floor (13th) of the hotel. First class Charlie, as Sarge calls him.

His very large (1,200 square feet) suite costs $1,700.00 per night, however, he got a big discount because he told the very sharp manager that he was a friend of Philly Police Chief, Leann Anderson.

The suite had a full -service kitchen with all of the serving plates and utensils. It also had two large bedrooms plus three full baths. And King size beds in both bedrooms and plenty of towels, blankets and extra pillows as well.

There were no amenities that you could ever want in your hotel suite that were not included in Charlie's room. None at all. And if you wanted anything, anything at all, all you had to do was pick up the phone and ask for room service. Everyone at the wonderful hotel was gracious, kind and extremely cooperative.

Charlie, being cheap, lets call in like it is, alright, set up Sarge and Jan at the 'Kimpton Hotel Monaco Philadelphia. It was just as absolutely lovely as was the Hilton Hotel, however, just a little bit less expensive.

And you know ole Charlie, money talks, even small change. The Kimpton, however, has just as many wonderful amenities and concierge services. You name it and they had it.

So, Jan did not complain at all, she loved the place, but Sarge, being Sarge, said to Charlie, "Did I ever tell you that you are cheap my Hefa?" Charlie retorted, "Yes, as a matter of fact my niño (son) you have, many, many times."

Now back to the perp (perpetrator) who tried to and almost succeeded in killing Sarge, Jan and old Charlie.

He was only 5 foot-tall and weighted in about 99 pounds. Had big oversized blazing black eyes that never stopped moving. His neighbors told the Chief, that his eyes just kept moving from left to right and then right to left, constantly for some unknown reason.

They also said that he never talked just smiled, a scary, very scary smile at them. They were not at all surprised to find our that he had tried to kill some police officers. They added that they got the impression that he was a paid 'hit man' for some *terrorist* group from the Somalia, the Sudan or Yemen.

He was from Somalia, in North Africa, do you remember, '*Black Hawk Down*' (the Movie)? One of the finest war movies ever put on film, in Charlie's opinion anyway). It is a very, very dangerous place to visit, even if you are a 'cut-throat' and killer like this guy.

He came from the same town where most of the Merchant *Ship Pirates* live and take the ships to hold for Ransom. They get about Five- Million dollars per ship that they 'hijack'.

There are also lots of smugglers, despicable human trafficker's, identity thieves, hostage takers, and the like, in that same town.

Charlie told Sarge, “I hope and pray that you and I never have to go there on a mission or investigation, that place is a living and breathing cesspool and garbage dump.”

CHAPTER THREE

DOCTOR ANNE E. FORD, MD, was on the first flight that she could get out of the huge and bustling LA-X (*Los Angeles International Airport*). It is one of the biggest and busiest as well as safest airports in the whole wide world.

The LA-X by the way, has their own Police Department and its own Police Chief. And also, it has several hundred Police Officers patrolling it is just like protecting a small city. In reality, it is much bigger than a lot of cities in the state.

LA-X Chief of Police is *David L. Maggard*, Jr. He has 650 officers reporting to him, and it is one of the largest Police departments in California. He used to report to LAPD (Los Angeles Police Department), however, he now is independent of them and works directly for the LA-X Board of Directors.

Four of his outstanding Police Captains that he relies heavily on at LA-X are; Susan Lee Smith, in charge of *Terrorism* and Crowd Control, Sheri Maretsky, in charge of Public Relations, and Ray Feldherr, in charge of Traffic Control, *Don Kutz,* in charge of Airline Counters and Airline passengers safety and Thomas Rose is in charge of all of the thousands of advertisements, posted all over the airport.

By the way, *Thomas Rose* is an old friend of Charlies and he is one of Charlies *favorite* people in the whole world. He has a lovely and very intelligent wife, Pamela who is smarter than Thomas, but do not tell him that this writer said that, please do not.

Unfortunately, very unfortunately, Thomas is battling that 'hated' big C (*Cancer*). And has been doing so for the past few years. He is so brave and strong, and seldom complains about the intense 'pain and suffering' it causes him on a daily basis.

He is one of Charlies Heroes in life and Charlie drives down through the 'horrible' traffic to LA-X to have lunch with his old church buddy, as often as possible. Charlie wants Thomas to 'get well fast' and have a full and complete recovery, he truly does.

Charlie said that Thomas is one of the bravest and most dedicated men that he has ever met in his entire lifetime. Charlie just doesn't understand why 'bad things happen to good people.' He really doesn't.

Charlie told Sarge and Jan, that the LA-X Police department was founded in 1946, and has gone through lots of changes over the years just like every other law enforcement agency.

The Chief, Maggard, is a veteran of policing and is very highly regarded by fellow law enforcement agencies throughout the whole nation. He not only police's LA-X, however, he also runs the Security for the small but extremely busy Van Nuys Airport as well as the Ontario Airport (in Ontario, California).

The Chief does not just sit in his office like some other police chiefs do. He foot -patrols the whole hundreds of acres of air-port property. Also, he talks directly with airport passengers on a daily basis.

And, he is the first to confront a terrorist suspect with a weapon or a bomb, a drunken and disorderly passenger, and/or a 'high' airplane pilot who is unfit to fly. He is not afraid of hard work nor danger, at all, and also, he is dedicated to *protecting* the traveling public, he is fearless and

Van Nuys is where a lot of the 'Rich and Famous' people fly in and out of in their quite expensive private jets. They do not like the long delays at the big LA-X nor the huge amount of traffic getting in and out of the airport.

Brief history of Van Nuys Airport, Charlie told Sarge, "we need to look that up on the internet sometime, I have always been interested in the small but famous and well used little Van Nuys Airport."

Now, back to *Doctor Ford* who the best GP (General Practioner) in the OC (Orange County) as well as all of southern California. She was very well respected by all of her doctor associates, and colleagues, as well as all of her patients.

She always tells people that Charlie is her 'favorite' patient, and she loves him dearly, even though he "cry's like a big baby sometimes when he has been seriously injured (shot and/or stabbed)".

She was Charlie's personal physician and she has patched him up numerous times after he was shot and/or stabbed. She even traveled to the Middle East (Iraq) one time after he was injured and in critical condition and could not be sent home to California for proper medical care.

Doctor Ford works out of the excellent St. Jude/St. Joseph Medical Center in Fullerton, California. That is in North County of the OC. It is ranked as one of the top 10 Hospitals in all of California.

Sarge said to Charlie when he met Dr. Ford, "Charlie, wow, she is very intelligent, a great doctor, not to even mention that she is very pretty with great hair and great legs too."

Charlie quickly replied, "Careful my little sidekick, you are drooling, wipe your mouth, you look like a kid who just saw his piñata." And then added, "Where is your professionalism and self-control?"

Sarge snapped back, "For one thing, my over- the- hill PI, I do not have any self-control when it comes to pretty and smart women, I find them quite sexy. And two I was not drooling, you fool, I was just licking my lips."

Charlie continued, "Alright Sarge, just try to control yourself when you are around my personal doctor, OK?" Sarge, "Sure thing old man, I will try but I cannot make any promises, you know how we 'Latin Lovers' are, right?"

Doctor Ford, was called by Chief Anderson because the Chief knew the doctor from when she used to live in Yorba Linda, California.

Because Charlie was shot and injured, but not all that badly, thank Dios, and also Jan and Sarge were hurt and needed some urgent medical treatment and Charlie needed some TLC, naturally

Charlie O'Brien is a Dreamer, he truly is, and he has been one ever since he was a little kid in rural Ojai (Ventura County, California). He was born in downtown Los Angeles, then his parents moved there, after which he grew up in the barrio in La Puente (San Gabriel Valley), California.

When he was small, he wanted to be a 'cowboy' like Hop-a-long Cassidy (Hoppy), or the Lone Ranger, the Cisco Kid, et cetera.

Then as a teenager he fell in love with the genre' of police detectives, private eyes, and private investigator. Such as Mike Hammer, Sam Spade, Magnum PI, Harry "Dirty Harry" Callahan (Clint Eastwood).

And The A-Team, Columbo, 77 Sunset Strip, Route 66, Horatio Caine, Miami Vice, Cannon, Nick Carter, Sherlock Holmes, Kojak, and Perry Mason.

Also, Hercule Poirot, Ellery Queen, Jim Rockford, and Spencer, amongst many, many other great Detective and Mystery TV shows that Charlie watched while he was growing up.

Today, he dreams that he is Jason Strathan, Liam Neeson, Clint Eastwood, Duane 'The Rock' Johnson, Chris Hemsworth, Kurt Russell, Jackie Chan, or Arnold Schwarzenegger, depending upon the dream he was having.

Charlie is one of the few true-life *fearless* Detectives in America or so I have been told. He uses his personal and extensive experience which is based upon his solid daily work ethic and personal beliefs, as well as his background of a twenty (20) year career with the LAPD (the outstanding, Los Angeles Police Department).

He worked under the great Barnard 'Bernie' Parks, one of the *best* police chiefs ever in LA, next to William "Bill' Parker (whom the city named the Police Headquarters building after), *and*

Charles 'Charlie' *Beck*, also one of the most outstanding police Chief's that LA ever has had, of course.

He was a *'Robbery and Homicide* Detective' and he worked on the possessed *'Charlie Manson'* family case. As well as many other very high-profile murder cases in LA (Los Angeles). The madman Charlie Manson, just died recently in prison after being locked up for the past 40 years.

Our man, good *Charlie the PI*, always said that it was too bad that the State of California did away with the *death* penalty, which Manson was given for the brutal and senseless killing of several people back in 1969 LA.

Combined with his current ten years of being a PI (Private Investigator, or Private Eye as some prefer to call him), to investigate and then solve, very large *'White Collar'* crime cases in the USA as well as all over the Globe.

He finds that by putting his beliefs into action (putting his feet where his mouth is...so to speak) it gives him an edge in understanding, dealing with and then capturing heinous crooks and criminals of all kinds.

Charlie primarily investigates embezzlement cases in the so called 'too Big to Fail' Banks in the good ole US of A as well as in foreign countries located all around the world.

He also investigates serious criminal activities in *'Ponzi'* schemes (think Bernard L. 'Bernie' *Madoff* and his 65 Billion...yes Billion dollar rip off of the American public) and also unethical stockbroker/investment bankers Lehman Brothers, AGI, Manhattan Bank, the Old Merrill Lynch Corporation [now owned and operated by Bank of America].

And one of the worst of the worst, Country Wide Funding (which was located in the real estate capital of the world, California), et cetera, the list goes on forever. Charlie wants to find the executives from this evil and corrupt organization and put them in a black-ops prison in Europe.

And he also sometimes helps to solve other types of 'criminal' activities that occur in his beloved California, where he hangs his hat (lives). Some of these crimes include bank art theft robberies, kidnappings, crooked politician's shenanigans and bombings, just to name a few.

During Charlie's in-depth investigations as a PI, he frequently encounters some very scary *villains* and heinous and extremely dangerous *criminals*.

He uses his strong and honest beliefs, his devotion to duty, as well as relying on his very sharp mind to assist him in researching and then solving, his very challenging, and complicated, and usually quite dangerous cases.

^^^^^

Charles, albeit, his best friends, fellow Private Investigators (Private Eyes), and LAPD (Los Angeles Police Department) Detectives, and the OCSD (Orange County Sheriff's Department), just call him "*Charlie*." I want you to know that Charlie does *not* enjoy getting older, not one little bit.

As a matter of fact, he hates it... immensely. He truly does. People tell him, "Charlie, you look good for your age." Kind of a left-handed compliment would not you say?

He realizes that they are just trying to be kind, however, he wishes that instead, they would say to him: "Charlie, you're still tall, dark and handsome."

That would be a big lie but he would whole-heartedly buy into it. He really would. And, besides, he is still tall, and one-out-of-three isn't bad, right?

He tries and tries, but he just cannot stop good old father- time from marching across his handsome (he wishes) face. In addition, most of his previously nice dark black hair is now turning gray. At least he still has all *of his hair*, thank *God*!

A lot of his friends are bald and they would kill to have gray hair rather than have no hair at all. Oh, well, we all have our crosses to bear in this crazy old world and his currently is that he just does not have the looks, nor the energy, that he did when he was in his prime.

Charlie now lives in Beverly Hills, California (just west of downtown Los Angeles) which some people call La-La Land. They are incorrect though, LA is "the City of Angels" ...it is 'Hollywood' that is really called La-La Land, trust me on that.

He was born and raised here and he most likely will die here...maybe one day soon...you just never know when you will be run over by a big RTD bus or a 400-horse power Dodge Charger (OCSD or a LAPD, police cruiser) chasing a gangbanger in a stolen Mercedes Benz 500S; or even worse, hit by one of the new red-blue-yellow train lines now crisscrossing LA like a scrabble board (or falling dominos).

He actually lives in *Beverly Hills*, California, close to the majestic and royal blue *Pacific* Ocean. That lovely and one of the most expensive cities to live in located in the United States, is close to the famous city of Huntington Beach (Surf *City*, USA).

Remember the Beach Boys? Some of them recently performed at the LWV Performing Arts Center. Charlie was told by some residents that it was just an absolutely fabulous concert. They sang 'Surfin USA' and a lot of elderly people got up and busted a move.

Now back to the *action*, Charlie called in another favor from another Private Detective and old friend of his, *Natalie Holm*.

He needed her to do some additional background checks on the many potential suspects and 'gangs' that might be behind the Philly 'crime wave.

Charlie called Natalie from his lovely and spacious penthouse suite at the Hotel by the River on his satellite and encrypted cell phone, that never, ever left his person. She answered right away, recognized his number, and spoke, "Charlie, old man, how is it going? Long time no talk, thought maybe the bad guys finally got to you."

And then, "By the way how is your good looking and strong sidekick, Sarge doing?" Charlie, laughed and then laughed some more. "Very funny Natalie, very, very funny, ha, ha, do you see me laughing?"

Followed by, "You know that you think that I am better looking than Sarge, and you also know that I am smarter than him, right? Natalie." Natalie laughed and then laughed some more, "Charlie, I Love you dearly, but you are 100 years old and you just are not as hip as Sarge, and you know it."

Charlie, "Alright Natalie you have had a good laugh at my expense, now let's get down to business, or brass tacks as Sarge always says. I need some of your internet and background check expertise on the case we are working on in Philly. Also, I may need you to fly up here in a couple of days. Do you think that you could do that for your old boss from the LAPD?"

Charlie had told Sarge about Natalie before and this is what he had told him. "Natalie is only about 4'11" and around 99 pounds, she has a great figure and pretty long red hair, and Sarge you know that I love redheads, right?"

Then he added, "She looks like she is about 23 and just out of San Diego State University. She is a Private Detective but also a part time attorney. She lives in the absolutely lovely San Diego bay area over-looking magnificent *'Coronado Island'*, that is where a lot of US Navy ships and personnel are located."

The lovely Island used to be all Navy however, the US Government has sold a lot of the land to developers who have built a lot of beautiful Condominiums there. Then Charlie continued, "Natalie knows Karate and Tae Kwon Do and other martial disciplines."

"Yes, small and petite but she can fight like a Pit-Bull, but only when she has too. Also, she is street smart and very well education. Her nice husband is also a part-time attorney and part time PI."

Charlie told Sarge, "Natalie is a surfer-girl and she still likes to 'hang-ten' out in the nearby royal blue Pacific Ocean. And she can swim all the way to Coronado Island and back without any problem."

Natalie to Charlie, "I am on it my good old friend. I will call you back with some good stuff on your perp's asap. Also, Charlie, "Watch your back in Philly, I hear that they have some really *bad dudes* in the 'City of Brotherly Love."

Then she added quickly, "Tell Sarge that I think he is better looking and smarter than you are, then laughed, and continued, "And next time you and your lovely model wife are down this way, lets all four go on a 'Surfin Safari' together, alright?"

Charlie's turn to laugh, "Sure Natalie, she would love that and she thinks the world of you just as I do. And no, I will not tell Sarge what you said, because you know that I am much better looking and much smarter than he is."

CHAPTER FOUR

ON WEEKENDS CHARLIE drives his Classic 1964 *Chevy Impala* two-door hardtop. This beautiful ride has been completely restored to the original condition. He just loves classic cars and he has owned several of them over his life time.

His Impala is the Super Sport model with a large big-block 409 cubic inch V - 8 HO [high output] *engine,* 4 on the floor stick *transmission* with a deluxe chrome knob shifter. It also has Posi traction non-slip rear end differential and original Cragar *magnesium* wheels from the 1960's.

It has very large and comfortable black leather bucket seats and it is original deep maroon in color. The engine is all chrome as well as the whole undercarriage.

The whole car is in pristine and mint condition, it truly is. It appraised for around $75,000.00 recently, however, Charlie would never sell his baby. It is part of his persona and makes him feel young once again whenever he takes it for a spin.

Every time Charlie drives his baby around LA or the OC on weekends all of the old guys and gals and even lots of young people, give him a thumbs-up. Sometimes they even say, "*Old guys with old cars rule*."

Charlie liked that comment so much that he went out and had several T-shirts made with that saying printed on the back of them. He does not like T's with writing on the front, just on the back for some unknown reason. Some of them are navy blue but most of them are white, naturally.

The other day as Charlie dressed for work, he looked into the mirror. Staring back at him was an extremely handsome angular man, around six feet four with a surfer mop of Pacific Ocean sun-kissed hair. He had preternatural hazel eyes...so intense that whenever most women looked at him...they had to avert their eyes in embarrassment.

Well, to be truthful, at least his eyes *are* hazel, but hardly any women starred at him any longer. He took *another* look, just for fun, and he saw a good-looking man with an angular face topped by a nest of naturally wavy black hair.

And a shy smile, albeit Charlie is anything but shy, that made women *swoon*...so boyish and charming, yet masculine at the same time. You dreamer you!

He had a six-*pack* courtesy of crunches and weight lifting at 24 Hour Fitness and a very strict eating regimen. Then, finally he realized that he was just *imagining* what he saw in the little mirror.

So, he decided to take another look...a harder look this time and he saw his real self, he thought anyway. Sometimes our man Charlie gets mixed up with which mirror.

Appearing in his mirror was a very nice looking, mature gentleman with a full head of hair, albeit some of it was grey, we'll all right, a lot of it.

With friendly-warm yet piercing *hazel* eyes, that sometimes looked blue, other times looked green (Irish eyes are shining) and sometimes even looked brown.

He did not see a six-pack this time around (frown) nor a smile that would make women swoon, sorry Charlie but you have to know your limitations I am sorry to tell you.

All-in-all, what he saw this time was a man who had lived a very hard life, always worked hard, always tried to help others who were less fortunate than himself and always tried to do his best at whatever task he had before him.

Then he said to himself, out loud as usual, "Charlie, you're the man!" Then, he turned and left the bathroom with the image of the first man he saw in the mirror, still in his mind's eye.

Do you remember that great old 'Motown' song, "Charlie Brown" by the fabulous *Coasters*? Charlie just absolutely loves 'Barry Gordy's *Motown* Music', he truly does.

Charlie and his lovely model looking wife, just saw the fabulous *'Smokey* Robinson' at the Cerritos [a quite marvelous venue Charlie says] Performing Arts Center in southern California.

It was just an unbelievable performance, and just to make it even more *memorable*, Mr. Barry Gordy [yes, himself] was in the audience. How cool was that. Smokey and Barry live in the same theater. Wow.

Do you remember some of the fun lyrics, "Charlie Brown who walks into the classroom real cool and slow, and calls the English teacher, Daddy-O. And why's everybody always pickin' on me."

"Who's always goofing in the hall, guess who? Yeah, you, Charlie Brown." This amongst tons of other great Motown songs were written by Mike *Stoller* and Jerry *Leiber*, two of the great Rock and Roll songwriters of all time, in Charlie's mind.

Well Charlie has a great sense of humor, he got it from his beloved mama. He loves to laugh and tell funny, and sometimes they are true, stories.

However, some of his fellow Private Detectives, and OCSD, LAPD officers amongst many others, love to sing, "Here comes

Charlie Brown" whenever they see him after a long period of time.

Some people say that Charlie is a pessimist, but that is just not true. Actually, he used to be a consummate optimist, but he has never been a pessimist, ever.

A glass half-full kind of guy. as they say, however, that was before all of the many 'trials and tribulations' in his life. Also, no, he has said my glass is almost empty.

He now days, says, my glass is half-full and half-empty. That is how the realist looks at things in this crazy-old mixed-up world that we live in. Life has a way of changing your perspective your life, over time. It truly does.

In addition, our man Charlie likes things simple, really simple and the simpler the better. He subscribes to that age old saying, "KISS" [keep it simple stupid].

Life today is way, way too complicated for him. For one thing he does not understand computers, at all. When he was a kid, they had manual adding machines, and then along came the electric versions.

He used them all of the time and loved them. Even still has some laying around. He also used to be so smart and quick that he did lots of calculations in his head.

He is not exactly sure, but he cannot do that anymore. Old age, early dementia, perhaps. His cell phone is also somewhat of a mystery to him. It is almost like a tiny, small computer these days.

Someone said to him recently while on an investigation, not a very nice person by the way, that he was *high*-tech challenged. He would have been quite offended, but he was not sure what they meant. So, he just smiled.

Also, he does not know much about the Internet, nor computer software for that matter. Just the other day he heard that he was on the 'dark web' whatever that is?

Bad he knows, but how did he get there and where is it located? In Europe or the far east?

Charlie is going to Call Jan Smoker and have her explain to him all about the Dark Web and how to get off of it. And also find out who put him on it, and then take care of them.

And the terms and definitions for computers as well as their software, confuse him greatly. Such as giga-bites, or terra bites, or thumb drives, RAM, different processors, all-in-ones and on and on.

He is planning on taking a computer class from Barbara *and* Craig *Harris*, at the LWV PC workshop to understand the nuances of the computer world that his old school private eye finds himself living it.

Furthermore, Charlie is a *dreamer*, and he dreams of a world completely void from all 'evil and heinous' criminals. All types of bad guys and bad gals [Charlie says that there are lots more bad men in this nutty world than there are bad women, by far].

White collar ones, terrorists, murderer's, child molesters, identity thieves, crooked bankers and investment brokers. drug dealers, pornographers, con-artists and gypsies, dishonest arms dealers, crooked and lying politicians, just to name a few.

Wow, what an absolutely fantastic world that would be, would it not? See I told you that he was not a pessimist. He longs for a better, simpler and crime-free life style.

Just like Jurassic Park, without all of the big and mean and scary dinosaurs. People would help other people, the rich would help the poor, and people would love one another like family.

Yes, it is quite true that, that kind of America *and* world, would put him out of a job (being a Private Detective and all), but he could always go back to being a teacher.

Charlie had a very dysfunctional childhood due to an alcoholic and abusive father. Luckily for him, his beloved mama was a real-life saint.

He was born in downtown LA (*Los Angeles*) in what is now Korea-town (Pico and Olympic boulevard) and was raised in a poor and gang 'barrio' in La Puente, California.

Again, luckily, he grew up with the gang members [some from the infamous 'White Fence' East LA gang] and they liked him, he made them laugh they said.

So, they did not stab him with their *'switchblades'* nor shoot him with a *'zip-gun* like they did the other white kids in the neighborhood. Do you recall switchblades and zip-guns from back in the day?

Also, Charlie could speak a little (piquito) Spanish and they appreciated and liked that. He also liked Latino girls and they liked that about him too. He was not prejudiced like a lot of the other white kids.

To this very day, he is still not biased towards others of different nationalities and still loves Latino people. They all treated him like one of their own when he had no kind of home life and fed him many times when he was hungry.

Charlie tells people that the only things that helped him survive his rough childhood was his love for *'Rock* N' *Roll'* music:

Elvis Presley [the King of Rock N' Roll],

Carl Perkins, [the architect of Rock N' Roll]

Jerry Lee Lewis [the Killer],

Chuck Berry [the Fabulous One]

Johnny Cash [the King of Country],

Buddy Holly [the Original One],

Everly Brothers [the Harmony Twins],

Richie Valens [the San Fernando Valley Kid],

amongst many others, way, way too many to list herewith.

And his love for the *American automobile*. Well, alright if you insist, also his love for girls. He had his first girlfriend in the third grade.

She came right up to him on the corner and kissed him on the lips. Wow, he was hooked on the prettier and smarter sex from then on out.

As an adult, Charlie still loves cars, new BMW's but of course Classic cars of his youth so to speak. When he used to 'cruise' Bob's Big Boy drive-in restaurant with car-hops (do you remember those great old days) in *Pasadena* and also in *Whittier*, California.

Also, the A and W Root Beer drive-in restaurant in West *Covina*, California (San Gabriel Valley). At both Bob's and the A & W, he would see some of the hottest and fastest cars in southern California. The boys and girls would come from miles away just to 'make the scene'.

Charlie, would look at these fabulous rides and drool, and then he would dream of one day having one just like them. He never did get a Hot-Rod, however, he has had some Fly- cars later on in his life.

Charlie's first car was a used 1949 Chevy (Chevrolet as he likes to call them) Deluxe model four door sedan. He put a racing cam shaft in it and also put triple-carb's (carburetors) on top of the engine.

He lowered it in front for a Rake look, some of his Mexican friends were 'low-riders' and they lowered their cars in the back. He put on dual-pipes (exhaust) and moved the stick shift from the steering column to the floor.

It was just a six (cylinder) engine, however, when he was done with it, he could beat other fast Chevy's and Ford's with big V - 8 engines, at the Drag Strip's in Irwindale, or Pomona, California.

Also, he put in white 'tuck n' roll' upholstery in the back window, and on the seats and new Naugahyde lining on all of the doors. It was light blue in color.

He wanted to buy a newer and faster Chevy two door sedan, with a big engine, but just did not have the money since he was poor and had to work really hard just to get enough money for his one.

Charlie has always been and is still to this day, a Chevy man. He does not know why, he just is. Fords, Chrysler and some foreign cars are alright, but he likes to say, "If you are going to race, go Chevy V - 8".

He bought this older but hot set-of -wheels the day he turned 16 years old. When he turned age 17, he bought another Chevy (of course), a used 1956 Model 210 two door coupe with a small-block 265 V - 8 engine.

It was two-one in color, aqua and white and he dearly loved that ride. It had a three-speed stick on the column and once again he moved it to the floor. He always preferred floor shifts for some unknown reason.

He also added dual exhaust, again just as with his last Chevy. He says that if he still had that car today, it would be worth about $35,000.00. He paid $500.00 dollars for it back in the day.

Charlie has found out over the years that Classic cars [from the 1950's to the 1970's] are not only fun to 'cruise around' on the weekends, but they are also excellent investments.

For example, a 1957 Chevy Bel-Air two door hardtop coupe, in original mint condition, is worth around $100,000.00. It only cost about $1,500.00 or less back when it was new. That's inflation folks.

1953 1/2 Chevy Corvette = $500,000.00

1963 1/2 Ford Mustang convertible = $400,000.00

1970 Ford Mustang 'standard coupe' = Cost new about $5,000.00 and now is worth $25,000.00.

^^^^^

Charlie these days drives nothing but BMW's, the "*Ultimate Driving Machine*". The best made production vehicle in the world, in his opinion anyway.

He currently owns two of them. He would have more of them, several different models and such as well as more Classic Cars, if he had more room in his garage.

He is thinking of building a bigger garage next to his house to make room so that he can buy more cars. As I already told you, Charlie loves cars, old cars, fast cars any kind of car, he truly does.

A new BMW *750* iL Active Hybrid luxury sedan with a 455-horsepower engine and it goes zero to 60 in 4.7 seconds, that is fast folks. It is jet black, of course.

Charlie loves fast cars and he always has. Not so much racing type sports cars, but production vehicles with big and powerful engines. An absolutely beautiful and fabulous ride according to him.

The license plate on this BMW reads 8BAD986 [8 Bravo, Alpha, Delta niner, eight, six = in Military code]. He wants people to know that he is a *bad* dude (at least in his own mind, of course).

And also,

A new BMW M6 class with a big V - 8 engine and rear wheel drive. Charlie prefers rear wheel drive cars better than front wheel drive. He says that they handle better when you drive them fast.

It has almost neck-*breaking* speed, and it does almost 200 miles an hour on the famous *Audubon* in *Germany*. It has a great 8-speed automatic transmission that you can drive just like a stick shift, if you want to.

It has a hard top that folds neatly up into the trunk of the car. That makes it a cool convertible in the summer time and nice and warm with no rain or wind in the winter.

It also has Black Sapphire Metallic paint, with Aragon custom handmade brown leather seats. Also, it has deluxe 17" BMW alloy wheels, Bluetooth, and a high-tech navigator system.

The license plate number on this BMW reads "IM PRVTI" [as in I am a Private Eye]. Charlie has wanted to be a PI since he was a little kid growing up in East LA and the El Monte/La Puente barrio.

Some people say that *our man*, Charlie, has the sharp eye of a Falcon, or an *Eagle* (like *Swoop* the *Philadelphia Eagle* mascot perhaps), and a truer aim with a pistol, or an automatic rifle, you will never find.

Also, they say that he was very well thought of by the Police, the CIA and his fellow private detectives. They went on to add that he never asked them to do anything that he would not do himself, nothing at all.

The people in this very dangerous line of work, Law Enforcement, et cetera, notice things like that, they truly do. Charlie, they said was always the first man 'through the door' of the bad guys locations.

And the first person to get shot at or even take a bullet. Most of these former, and present, associates of his always did their best to support him and watch his back whenever they went into battle (got into a gun firefight).

He had been in many quite dangerous and precarious and life-threatening situations with Howard from the CIA, John from the FBI, LAPD Police Chief, Charlie (another good guy named,

Charlie), amongst many, many other Detectives *and* Private Eyes and even some famed Navy Seals.

All of them down to the very last one, said that Charlie was such a good role model of the 'good guys' that they would always do their utmost for him and even give up their lives for him if necessary.

Also, he was the first to come to the aid of another agent or operative, who was in trouble or wounded on a mission. And that he was one of the bravest people that they had ever worked/served with.

All of them said that they would follow Charlie anywhere, anytime and anyplace, and they sounded like they meant it, they really did. He always encouraged the new recruits, new agents and operatives, always.

Now, if you were to ask Charlie about these 'glowing' and very generous compliments, he will tell you and me, that they are not true or that they were overrated.

And that the men and women who made such very gracious comments about him were the real *'hero's'* and not him. Charlie is actually a modest guy, albeit, you would never guess that by the way he carries himself while on the job.

Also, he would add to that statement, that those kind people were just as brave and courageous as he was, and probably even more so. Well, definitely more so, he would add.

Charlie has been shot, as well as stabbed, several times over the years while doing his very dangerous and risky vocation as a Private Investigator.

That is to say, being a LAPD Robbery and Homicide Detective, a covert operative for the CIA and the FBI, the NSA, the OCSD, and working on quite death-defying cases involving some of the most evil and hardened criminals in the world.

And he always adds a true, however, very odd sounding comment, he says that he does not mind being wounded nor hurt "on -the- job". Little bit of a funny statement does you not think?

In addition, he says that the way he looks at it, getting injured is just an occupational hazard, that's all it is. Very similar to a construction worker losing a finger, or his big toe.

Or a firefighter [fireman and/or firewoman] getting burned in a raging fire while rescuing men, women, children and their beloved pets from certain death.

Or, a doctor or nurse, who catches a serious (and sometimes even deadly) illness from a very sick patient. Or, people that work in factories and foundries who lose arms, legs or their lives.

Or a banker who gets shot, or stabbed, during a bank 'hold-up', or placed and locked in the bank vault without any ventilation. Or, any number of other vocations [and there are more than you think] that carry with them the risk of injury or death.

Funny but the only thing that Charlie ever complains about is not being hurt at the office [kidding] but the time in the hospital critical care center or the long recovery time when he gets home. That's all.

He hates that the most, he says. And he cannot wait to get back 'on the streets' to investigate, and then to solve some more heinous 'White Collar' crimes somewhere in this crazy mixed up world of ours. Just anywhere on the globe is fine with him.

Just like the fearless moderator, John Walsh, of 'America's Most Wanted' real life TV show (was on Fox network for years, but now is on CNN), Charlie wants to be out there *'looking* for the *bad* guys'.

John and Charlie both say, "Here in the good ole US of A, as well as all over the entire world". Both of them have traveled thousands of miles around the globe searching for and locating evil crooks and criminals. They truly have.

Absolutely nothing in this world makes Charlie happier than when he locates, arrests, and sees them convicted in a Court of Law. It makes him ecstatic, it really does.

And then after that, see them put in captivity in a dark *hole* somewhere. And he always adds, preferably in a horrible and deplorable '*third* world' prison.

Charlie loves to teach. He used to teach *law enforcement* classes at both Cal- State University and Fullerton Community College in Fullerton, California at one time.

He still holds a Life-Time Teaching Credential from the Department of Education in Sacramento, California. And when he semi-retires from being a Private Eye, he is planning on going back to teaching at Saddleback Community College in the OC or Cal-State University Fullerton.

Charlie is a big strong and very tough guy, but he is also very gracious at the same time. And he always laughs when he hears someone say, "Here he comes, our man Charlie Brown" and gives a big old *smile* too.

In real life, his Lucy is his lovely wife, Lynn. Lucy in the cartoon is cute, albeit, his *Philly* girl, looks like a model, she truly does.

CHAPTER FIVE

"THE CITY OF BROTHERLY LOVE", Charlie said to Sarge, and added, "Now let me tell you a little history to help educate you my favorite, yet not well educated niño." And then he continued, "This is what you would have learned about in history class had you not been staring at all of the pretty girls."

Sarge grumbled, and retorted, "You are just jealous because none of the girls in your history class paid you any attention, so you had nothing else to do but listen to the teacher, who as I recall you said was 'smoking' hot."

Charlie's turn, "Well as a matter of fact nosey one, she was smoking hot, just 22 years old and I think that she had a thing for me, if I had been older, of course." Then he thought and added, "Boy Sarge, I wish I had been 22 also. Oh well, a man can dream, can't he?"

Sarge's turn, "Sure Charlie, that is all old men like you can do, dream about the good old days."

Finally, Jan broke in, again, and said, "Enough you two, you remind me of *'Stan Laurel and Oliver Hardy'.* But I am not quite sure which of you is Laurel and which of *your is Hardy?"* And, then she added, "Now, Charlie let's get *back to your history* lesson on 'The City of Brotherly Love, Philadelphia, alright?"

Philadelphia, Pennsylvania

Nickname(s): "Philly", "The City of Brotherly Love", "The Athens of America", and other nicknames of Philadelphia

Motto(s): "Philadelphia maneto" (Let brotherly love endure or continue")

Founded in 1682

Founded by William Penn

Elevation: 39 ft (12 m)

Population (2018): 1,584,138

Rank US city: 6th

Time zone: UTC-5 (EST), Summer (DST), UTC-4 (EDT)

ZIP codes: 19092-19093, 19099, 191xx

Area codes: 215, 267, 445

Major airport: Philadelphia International Airport

Website: www.phila.gov

William Penn, an English Quaker, founded the city in 1682 to serve as capital of the Pennsylvania Colony. Philadelphia played an instrumental role in the American Revolution. Philadelphia is the birthplace of the United States Marine Corps.

After these very interesting facts about the 'City of Brotherly Love', Philly, Charlie continued his dissertation to Sarge. Charlie's lovely long-legged wife, who looks just like a model, was born just outside Philly, in Coatsville, Pennsylvania.

She was raised across the famous *'Delaware River'* just into New Jersey. Where the famous Little Stevie, of the E-*Street* Band lead by the Boss (**Bruce Springsteen**) "this is not Heaven, you fool, it is New Jersey."

Since she was from that area, she obviously knew a lot more about Philly than Charlie and the rest of his A-Team investigators. Charlie checked out the internet, you can find out about any place on earth there and fast, real fast.

Of special note, Charlie told Sarge, "Philly was the first Capital of the United States of America. Most people do not know that, they think that the Capital was always in Washington D.C."

Actually, Charlie had visited Philly and several people he used to know who lived in that area, back in the day (1980'). He absolutely loved all of the quite beautiful and historic buildings in 'The City of Brotherly Love.'

They have the famous Liberty Bell there, plus more historic places to see than you can even imagine. Also, it is where they filmed one of the *greatest* boxing movies ever made, 'Rocky' with Sylvester 'Sly' Stalone.

Charlie told Sarge that the people in Philly are 'very different than the people in Southern California. They are much more direct, he said. They like to tell it like it is and they do not beat around the bush. They call that kind of speech, "Keeping it real." They also call it, having a little '*attitude*.'

They are usually always in a hurry, not real patient, do not like waiting in lines, and also, they are not real politically correct. Charlie told Sarge, "You notice that I am always easy going, very patient and politically correct, right?"

Sarge could hardly contain himself, and immediately spit out, "Charlie, old man, what are you talking about? You are not that patient, at all, nor are you always politically correct either."

Then Sarge opened his mouth again, while he was still laughing at his own little jest, "Also, Jefa, you generally always say what you think even if it makes an enemy." Big laugh from Charlie, and then an even bigger laugh.

Charlie replied, "Well Sarge you really know how to hurt a guy's feelings." Laughed, again and then continued, "Listen to me my little opinionated Latino son, you are correct but you do not need to tell the whole world about some of my many 'flaw's, do you?"

Charlie added more, "You, by the way, Mr. Tubbs of Miami Vice, have a few character flaws as well." Charlie thought for a brief moment, then continued, "Take for example, you always criticize me for not being 'politically correct', but also very strongly express your personal opinions too, just saying Sarge."

Sarge then looked at Charlie cocked his head to the side, and said, "Go on old man, you're, on a roll." And Charlie did, after he took a deep breath, "Also, my shorter than me, little 'protégé' you talk too much. Jabber, jabber, jabber all of the time."

Charlie, more, "Sometimes I cannot get a word in edge-wise." Sarge retort, "Thanks for sharing Jefa, and I hope that you feel better now, also I appreciate your candor and I want you to know that I will immediately forget it, all of it."

Sarge added, "Now that we are in Philly investigating a dangerous 'crime wave', 'look at another mess that you got me into', my Stanley Laurel personage." Then Charlie chuckled and then Sarge continued.

"Charlie, I love you like a Latino brother but, you are always getting me into big, big, 'messes' and sometimes even almost getting me killed." Then he laughed at his own humor, and said, "Sarge you got that line from the old *vaudeville* comedy duo Stan Laurel and Oliver Hardy, didn't you? Copycat."

Charlie took a short breath, and then went on, "Sarge, you cannot even come up with an original funny line by yourself. You love to copy other people's lines like, Riggs and Mautha from *Lethal Weapon*, Jackie Chan and Chris Rock from *Ride Along* and *Sonny* Crockett and *Ricardo* Tubbs from *Miami Vice*."

Here was Sarge's retort, "Well, yes OK my senile boss, I use other famous comic's funny lines, but you cannot even remember their lines. *Dementia*. I think that they call that loss of memory my friend."

Charlie ended the discussion, finally, "Enough niño, let's get back to the much more important case at hand, The City of Brotherly Love 'crime wave' alright Sarge?" Sarge always the one to get the last word in, "OK my *senior* citizen, but just remember, I was the one who won this friendly little argument, as usual."

Charlie, just laughed and then shrugged his shoulders, and laughed some more, and then without saying another word, he just turned his back to his BBF, Sarge.

And then he said to OCSD *Sergeant, Kevin Lybrand*, "You newcomer to our 'good ole boy club,' you come with me. I think that I will leave him here for a little while to reflect on his erroneous thinking about me." And then Charlie headed back to his prearranged meeting with Philly Police Chief, Leann Anderson.

CHAPTER THREE

CHARLIE ASKED SARGE, "My favorite niño, with the big *mouth*, who are the most logical 'suspects' for the quite severe crime wave here in Philly that you, Howard and Jan, both retired CIA, have come up with so far."

His response, "Well, my senior citizen boss, with *dementia*, here is the list that I made up for you and the rest of our A-Team, and the Philly Chief of Police, to review."

Then he, continued, "Some are more viable suspects than others, however, I have *whittled* the list down to just these few perps from a much larger, and longer list."

Added, "With the kind and needed assistance of Natalie Holm, the very sharp and fearless PI from San Diego, I was able to eliminate a lot of innocent, probably, suspects so that we could concentrate on the most probable losers."

And now, more *banter* from our comedy duo, Charlie and Sarge. Sarge to Charlie, "My wise ole Jefe, why do you think that there are so many bad guys, and gals, in this crazy mixed-up old world that we live in?"

Charlie pondered, that deep question, and after some time chewing on it, so to speak, he finally answered, "I personally think my little, short Latino son, that there has always been just as many bad people, both men and women, in the world since it first began about 10,000 years ago. But with the internet, and 24/7 news channels, we are made more aware of them than back- in -the- day."

Now for Sarge's response, "My trusted Jefe, you are a very wise soul, indeed." Charlie, with a big grim all across his face, "I am so happy that you finally recognized that my loyal sidekick."

Sarge retort, "I always knew tat you were a smart guy, my mentor, I just think that you are over-the-hill and a little bit senile." Charlie fumed, and turned red in the face, and spit out, "What? Are, you, nut's, Sarge?"

Charlie took a deep breath, and then continued his *tirade*, "I am as sharp as, when I was 39 years old, and also I am twice as fast on the draw." Sarge knew how to get ole Charlie going, and when he was bored, he would say something silly just to stir him up, and just for the fun of it.

Finally, once our man Charlie, calmed down, at least a little bit, he said to Sarge, "OK, ok, my short legend in your own mind, niño, how about we go and catch some of the bad guys? That is if you have had enough fun harassing your BBF, that is?"

Sarge laughed, and then laughed some more, and spoke, "Sure old man, I have had enough fun for now, so let's go 'amongst them' once again just like King David did in the olden days."

Drive By- Shootings:

1. *MS-13* (El Salvadorian gang). The gang leadership in the Philly Chapter of the gang is listed herewith, the main leaders are still in El Salvador, Central America.

'Carlos Jose de Quintana,' nicknamed, the 'Hefa', or the Patronne. They say that he made people and even his rough and tough criminal associates, tremble when they were around him.

'Gonzalo (the Bull or El Toro) Pedro Garcia'. He put the fear of *Dios* into everyone he knew. He was as big as a bull, 6'6" and about 274 pounds and he loved to go to the bull fights in Mexico whenever he can get out of Philly. He told people that he wanted to be a Matador when he was a little kid, but people told him that he was way, way to big.

'Javier (the Horse) Fernandez Santiago'. People felt that he would stampede their heads into the ground at the drop of a hat. He looked mean, but he was in reality much meaner than he appeared.

'Alvaro (the Serpent or the Snake) Fernando Martinez'. He bites just like a Norte Americano sidewinder and his bite is quite deadly quite. He was little only 5'2" and 135 pounds, but was as violent as a 6'5" gang banger.

'Felipe (El Coache or car) Isidoro Carrillo'. He was called the Car because he ran over people faster than a brand- new Cadillac Escalade with a 454 engine, a new Z-71 Chevy Corvette with a HO racing engine, or a Chevy Camaro SS with a big block 350 V-8 engine, turbo charged and with a 6- speed stick transmission.

And, last but clearly not the least of this despicable group of cutthroats and gang- bangers from El Salvador,

'Alejandor (the Blade) Jorge Alvarez'. He was so lightning quick with his 10" knife that he cut people before they could even draw their own knives or guns. He had his favorite long knife on his side, a small 6" one on his ankle, and a longer 15" Machete slung across his back too.

These were the vicious and vicarious leaders of the MS-13, Philly chapter. They were all as dangerous as vipers in the desert and the rest of their Motley crew of killers, drug dealers, thugs, and gang bangers, were just as bad and also just as dangerous. Indeed.

MS-13 was one of the most vicious *and* deadly street gangs in the county. They also ran many of the prison gangs in the nation. They were even the 'shot callers' for *hits* (executions) 'outside' of the jails and prisons, as well as 'inside' of them.

The members were all from the very poor and crime ridden south American country of El Salvador. You probably remember the 'Contra-Costa' wars back in the day.

The country of El Salvador, Charlie knows lots of people from El Salvador, and he really likes them, a lot. He knew a lot of them from when he worked *'Rampart' Division* for the LAPD (Los Angeles Police Department).

He worked right next to the lovely little *MacArthur Park,* named after the famous World War II hero, General Douglas MacArthur (Jan. 26, 1880 to April 5, 1964). It was located very close to the corner of 6th Street and Alvarado Street, in LA. It is one of the most crime- ridden and gang- infested parts of LA.

Charlie's beloved *mama* used to take him to that very same little man-made Lake when he was a just a little kid. It was very nice and safe back in the day, his mom told him when, he became to be a LAPD Cop.

But most all of the El Salvadorian people are very nice, clean, and honest individuals. With the exception of the 'gang bangers', but even some of them liked our man Charlie.

They would say, "Hey, *homes*, what's happing?" When they saw him in his police- cruiser? They were always unmarked, and all black, of course. They gangs could spot them for miles. They had lots of antenna's and blue and red lights hidden in the grills and also in the rear panel by the back windows.

"You better not let me catch you 'slipping' my amigo, or I will run your butt into the *Rampart Police* Station, you feel me, dog?" Then he would laugh and so would they. They knew that ole Charlie would not bug or bust them unless they did something really, really bad.

Some of the local LAPD officers were into just harassing them even when they had not done anything wrong. Charlie treated them with respect, and because of that, they treated him the same way. They also would give him good 'intel' about what was going down in their 'hood.'

2. *Rolling 60 Crips* [they always wear *blue* headbands on their foreheads]. The original leaders came to Philly from South Central LA [Los Angeles, California] back in the day. Charlie knew that area real, well as he used to patrol that rough area when he was a Rookie for the LAPD.

The head 'Shot Caller' for the Philly branch of the Crips, was Humberto 'El Chapo' Escobar El-Sinaloa. Deadly as a poisonous

'Mohave Desert' California *Rattlesnake*. Charlie hates snakes, deadly or not, he hates them. All of them.

He stepped on one when he was a kid up at the 'Mammoth Mountain' Resort, in the High Sierras by *Bishop*, Lake Tahoe and Reno (the littlest big city in America), by the River, and it almost scared him to death.

3. *West Philly Bloods* [they always wear *red* bandana's headbands], their honchos were 'Straight out of Compton.' Charlie also used to work in Watts for the LAPD. And he told Sarge they were the nicest and most hospitable people in LA.

Minus the 'gangstas', of course. They would say, "Yo Charlie, bro break some bread with us when you are on your lunch break, home boy." They never shot at him as they do a lot of the LAPD cruisers and officers. His nickname in the Hood, was "Big White Boy." He liked that, liked it a lot.

The, people in Watts, knew that deep down inside, Charlie, was part Black. And he was *proud* whenever he heard someone called him Black. Charlie tells people, when they ask what nationality he is, he always tells them, "I look 'Anglo' on the outside, but, on the inside, I am part *Latino*, part Black, part Korean, part Native American and part *Irish*!"

'Watts' is not an official City it is part of the large City of Compton. Charlie was in that area when the 'Watts Riots' occurred. He was still working for the LAPD at that time, and he assisted with traffic, crowd control and tried to stop some of the looting that was rampant during the confusion.

Once time he told Sarge, "You know Sarge, when I was there in the riots, no one shot at me, nor even yelled, or spit on me." The only people that I saw out stealing from the poor, local, black store- owners, were the 'gang bangers' and a lot of them were from 'outside' of the area.

The vast majority of Watts residents are good, honest, hard-working black people and now, some Latino, family people. It is located just south and east of downtown LA. It was all white when Charlie was a little kid, then it became mostly African-American and now a lot of nice people from Central and South America live there.

They did not care about the real causes for the riots, at all, they just wanted to make a fast-buck by stealing merchandise, and then pawning it for money for drugs and guns. Most all of the stores that they burned and looted belong to very nice, honest and hardworking black individuals.

4. *Muslin Brotherhood* [originally from and still based in Egypt]. Their real name is 'The Society of the Muslim Brotherhood'. They were formed in 1928 in Ismailia, and now operate out of Cairo, Egypt.

In 1948, right after World War II, the Egyptian government, cracked down on the 'Brotherhood' and that dislike and distrust exits to this very day.

Charlie told Sarge, "Did you ever want to go to Egypt and see the great *Pyramids* of the ancient Kings?" Sarge to Charlie, "Yes, I used to really badly, but they kill American's in the Middle East now, and for no reason."

Charlie back at Sarge, "Yes, I know but I still would really love to see King Tuts tomb and the others as well. I have no idea how they made them that big (gigantic) back in the day?"

Then he continued, "Also, my little afraid amigo, I would like mainly to go to **Israel**. I would feel much safer there, than any place else in the Middle East, because I am part Jewish." Sarge, "What, I did not know that you were part Jew?"

Charlie's reply, "Yes, although, I was not born a Jewish person (one of God's chosen people), but I converted to being one in 2001." Sarge, "Wow, that is so very cool, Jefa, I might do that one day myself. I have lots of friends on the OCSD department that are Jewish, and I like them all."

They operate in the political area but also in worldwide 'criminal activities' in order to pay back Qatar and Turkey's ISS (Internal Security Service) the money that they owe them. They had to borrow a lot of cash from them for the 'Arab Spring'.

The ring leader and supreme Cleric of the 'Brotherhood' is 'Mohammed Badie', he is a very intelligent and also a very devious and vicarious, individual. The 'Brotherhood' is considered a Terrorist Organization and outlawed in Bahrain, Egypt, Russia, Syria, Saudi Arabia, the UK and also the United States.

They do drive-by shootings to take over 'turf' in cities like Philly, New York, Miami, and Los Angeles. Then they can set up mosques to collect donations to funnel back to Cairo and Turkey.

Smash and Grab's:

1. *Bonano Mafia* crime family, originally from New York, Queens, and now controlled most of the crime in South Philly. They needed 'Tribute' Money to pay the New York 'Godfather' (John Godi, IV)] who was from Sicily, just off the coast of lovely and romantic Italy.

The '**Black Hand'** (and later called the 'La Costa Nostra', Birthplace was and it came from *Sicily*, in the early part of the last century (1900's).

Charlie was in fabulous and exciting Italy, in 1996 and also on the beautiful and captivating Island of *Capri*, just off the coast of Napoli (Naples in Italian). Right above Naples was the quite historical city of *Pompei* on 'Mount Vesuvius', that erupted in about 64 A.D. and killed thousands, and thousands of people.

Charlie told Sarge, "I could not believe my own eyes, when I visited the still half buried in lava, City. It was like the town was stuck in time. People were going about their daily business and chores, and bam, bam, eruptions and then Death."

"It was a truly amazing place to visit Sarge, and if you ever decide not to be so cheap, you should buy a ticket, and go there. Sarge, "Maybe I will old timer, good thing you went back in the day, because you are too old and clumsy to go today."

^^^^^

2. *A Bank robber* who was accidentally released by the guards at a Metropolitan Correctional Center (Jail), in New York, where the despicable and *demon* possessed child molester, demon possessed and pervert, Jeffrey Epstein, hung (killed) himself. Saved us tax payers millions on his care, 3 hots and a cot, and appeals for year after year for the next twenty years, Charlie told Sarge, "May he rot in Hell."

Charlie, Sarge and the CIA, the DOJ (Department of Justice), and the FBI believe that one of the most nefarious and vitriolic and heinous human beings to have ever lived upon this planet, was Murdered and in reality, he did Not commit Suicide, at all.

Epstein had in his little 'black book' (actually on his encrypted lap top computer), his sexual customers for young, innocent and underage girls, names. A lot of these deplorable men, are some of the wealthiest and most influential men in the whole wide world.

Some foreign country Kings, billionaire Oil Sheiks, Past Presidents of the United States of America, William 'Billy Bob' Clinton and Donald T. Trump, at least that is what a friend at the CIA told Charlie and Sarge, in confidence, of course.

Many Hollywood A-Listed Movie and T.V. Producers and actors, as well as some of the wealthiest men anywhere on the Globe. You name the type of business, and somebody from that sector was a paying customer to the egregious criminal mastermind, and pervert, Jeffrey Epstein. May he burn in Hell, Charlie told Sarge.

3. A shotgun-packing and body armor wearing 'Meth-head' duo all the way from Southern California, Paul Peterson and Fred Lenscott, Jr. Theses two natural born losers were from the LA/ Orange County area.

The LAPD, LASD, RCSD, OCSD, OCDA, as well as the FBI were looking for them. Even the 'State Bar of California' were on the look-out for them. They apparently used to be flaky attorneys who embezzled money from clients and made a living evicting.

And, suing old people (elder abuse), widows and widowers, out on the street just because they complained to their HOA's (who these two crooks worked for) filed a lawsuit, and or complained about the HOA's to the local news media.

Peterson was younger about 40 or so, and very hyper-active, he had a severe case of ADHD, and he never stood still. He just kept shifting his weight from his left side to his right side and then back again.

He did this constantly and it drove his partner crazy. He also had a round-fat and dumb look on his face, most of the time, anyway. Lenscott, was the older of the two, the planner, always wore '*huarache*' beach sandals, everywhere he went.

He was an old-school *criminal*. Probably in his 70's now. Thinks he is a whole lot tougher than he really is. He is just a big bully Sarge told Charlie, "we at the OCSD know how to deal with big mean bullies who pick on, little kids, women, and the elderly, we really do."

Bank Robberies:

1. The *Nigerians*, who were into identity theft, kidnapping and holding for ransom, as well as bank robberies in foreign countries like the USA, the UK and Europe. Their gang name was the 'Flaming Sword.'

Nobody in poor Nigeria had any money to put into the banks for the gang to rob, so they had to go to other wealthier countries. The Capital of Nigeria is **'Abuja'**, and that was where the gang operated from.

They had complete immunity from the City, and Country officials and the Abuja Police as well. Charlie's A-Team and Sarge found out that the ring leader, of the 'Flaming Sword' was Usman dan Bahari.

He was worse than a sneaky big bad eel hiding in a reef in the Atlantic Ocean. Just waiting to size out and bite your hand off. When Usman came to the small and poor Nigerian towns and cities, the parents would hide their children in fear.

Next member was, Ms. Yemi Mullammda Saraki, and people called her the 'Mata-Hari' of Nigeria. She was easy on the eyes, Charlie was told. She was small, thin as most from that area, with pretty long very dark hair and eyes and full lips. She was all of 5' tall, with high heels.

Charlie said to Sarge when he saw the CIA's photo of her, that she would eat him for breakfast if he got even close to her. Next was, 'Bakola Fodio Osinbajo', he was Bahari's Lieutenant, as it were.

Also, quite small, 5'2" and only 110 pounds, with big hands for a small man, and an equally big mouth to match. He drank, smoke cigars, and gambled, all of which are forbidden in the Koran.

He would bet on anything that moved, they told Charlie. He had always said that some -day, when I got rich, he would come to the United States, to rob, cheat and steal from the ugly Americans.

He also bet on horse races, dog races, car races, prize fights, MFC Martial Arts contests, camel races and his favorite, soccer (fot-ball). He could not wait to get to the USA and Las Vegas (or Lost wages as Charlie calls it).

Then there was, 'Yakubu Nigeria Onnogen', who was a little bit taller than the average Nigerian. He was about 5'11' but only about 135 pounds. He was an expert at several martial arts disciplines.

He also was quite good at robbing people of their hard -earned money in crowds, airports and shopping centers. And also stealing their money on line with Identity Theft computer scams.

The last gang member was 'P. W. Nkanu Dogara', and his voice was like a husky whisper, quite deep for a very think man. Charlie asked Sarge, "Why do lots of bad men have real, deep and throaty voices?"

Sarge replied to Charlie this way, "They don't my old Hefa, they just make their high voices sound deeper to intimidate and scare people." Charlie, "O.K, I see Sarge."

He was very cunning and street -smart. Whenever he entered a room or a building, darkness, gloom and death seemed to follow right behind him. Charlie said, "If this guy is not a certifiable Sociopath, I have never seen one."

The people in Nigeria are very nice people, but they were so poor that they had to do anything they could do to survive and provide for their families. Many were orphans and were trained from a very early age to use the internet to defraud people in the United States out of millions and millions of dollars every year.

2. *Pink Panthers* [The original gangs grown- up kids]. They were Originally from the UK {United Kingdom and Ireland] and Western Europe (Serbia).

The original gang was international, old and very well financed and established. They were the King, the best bank robbers (as well as great jewelry store thieves) in the whole wide world.

The kids operated out of Brussels, Belgium in Europe, but they have teams of their members scouting the whole globe looking for easy marks. Banks and Jewelry Stores and Art Galleries for the gang to rob.

Several of the original *'Pink Panthers'* are dead or still in jail now. Their kids, however, are all grown up now and are seasoned crooks just like their parents and relatives were back in the day.

The ring leader was 'Olivera Vasic Cirkovic', she was Serbian and also part Russian. Her father was a Russian Communist soldier stationed in Yugoslavia during the cold-war when he met and married her mother who was a Movie Star.

Underneath her beauty and charm, was the heard of a predator Tiger. They say that she was part cat due to the way she moved, quick as a cat. Big wide and dangerous looking dark eyes and nice, very nice, curves to go with the rest.

Olivera was the type of woman who you never wanted to meet in a dark alley. Actually, you never wanted to meet her any place or at any time. He middle name should be 'Deadly Obsession' and she has buried many a good man in her day. Many.

The next criminal gang member was, 'Milan Popapoparic', he was a Serbian national and a close *relative* to the much hated and very evil, *'Marshall Josip Broz Tito.'* Tito was the 'despicable' Dictator and self-appointed President of the beautiful, old and former country of Yugoslavia from 1963 to about 1980.

Dictator Tito murdered, slaughtered, thousands of completely innocent men, women and children during his 'reign' of terror in Yugoslavia. People said that Milan, was crafty as a fox, and that he was excellent at scoping out potential Jewelry Stores, high-end Art Galleries and/or banks, for later robberies.

Also, that Milan to get in-and-out of any of these places of business 'faster' than a fox could get in-and-out of a hen house. Milan seemed like a pleasant person, albeit, when you got to know him, you found out that he was a 'stone cold killer.'

Then 'Boris Mermet', was also a Serbian but had a French family name. His family were at one time, very well known and quite wealthy Wine producers in France. He was a relative of "Slobodan Milosevic's the very *infamous* former Communist leader of Yugoslavia.

Besides being very god with a *Russian* made AK-47 automatic rifle, whenever he had too, he also could spring into action during a jewelry store, painting gallery, and/or bank robbery faster than a *cheetah*.

And people said that his voice was like a cat's *hissing* during a cat-fight. He also was quite good with C-4 (e.g. Malleable Plastique) Explosives. He has loved, just loved blowing things up ever since he was a little kid.

And last but clearly not least, of the New Pink Panthers' gang was 'Dragan Miklovic' and yet another Serb, he was a co-founder as well as a senior member of the New Pink Panther crime family.

He now, however, has to play second- fiddle to the newly promoted leader, 'Olivera Vasic Cirkovic'. He is the one who hired her, and trained her, but then she stabbed him in the back, so to speak, and took over his crew very vicariously.

He has blown most of his profits from his illegal activities with the Pink Panthers on all types of drugs, you name them, booze, he is partial to Russian *Vodka*, and women of the night.

He prefers to be called '*Dragon*' in-lieu of his real name, which is '*Dragan*.' It is said that he can pounce upon a jewelry store clerk or a bank teller/manager, in less than 60 seconds, during a robbery if he needs too.

3. *Mafia's 'Fat' Tony Gambino*. Philly mafia, and the great grandson of the infamous and nefarious Al Capone [SCARFACE]. Once thrown out of LA by the famous Police Chief William 'Bill' Parker just as he arrived from wind blown and freezing Chicago at the grand central train station in downtown LA.

The LAPD's main Police Station downtown LA, is named after Bill and it is called '*Parker Center*' in his honor. He was a totally fearless crime fighter and was not intimidated by anybody, including, deadly, *Scarface*.

Scarface, once the most *feared* criminal in the United States, and well protected by the City of Chicago's crooked politicians, was afraid to fly. He was a tough guy who had killed many people and 'had' several others murdered, but he was really just a big bully and scared to fly.

'Fat Tony's' real name was 'Anthony Alfonso Gambino'. He was actually tall and not all that fat. All Mafia members must have a 'nickname' and that just happened to be his. Actually, he thought it was funny because every time he met someone new, they would say to him, "I thought you were fat?"

'Fat Tony' has a wonderful daughter, *Betsy*, and she could swing a baseball-bat as good as any of Tony's 'crew.' She loved the color pink, and everything she owned was pink. She also, did have a few, purple items, as well.

She also loved pet house rabbits and she had one whose name was 'Nikki' and she had a nickname too, it was 'Busy.' That was because she was always getting into trouble and making a mess, therein, the name Busy.

Charlie has been to that old and historic station in LA several times over the years and a lot of TV shows and Movies have been filmed there over the years, as it is located right next to the famous "Hollywood", or 'La, La Land' if you prefer!

CHAPTER SEVEN

"PHILLY PD [POLICE DEPARTMENT] history" Charlie said loudly to Sarge. Now, "Open your ears my talkative compadre and you shall learn, something, hopefully although I know it is hard for you to listen and not talk."

Sarge alright my frustrated school teacher, and Hefa, go ahead and fill me in." Jan who was listening, as usual, said out loud, "Here we go again boys will be boys."

Both Charlie and Sarge laughed at her comment, but then immediately went back pranking each other. Charlie do you know what your problem is, boss?

In 2006, Philadelphia's homicide rate of 27.7 per 100,000 people was the highest of the country's 10 most populous cities. In 2012, Philadelphia had the fourth-highest homicide rate among the country's most populous cities.

The rate dropped to 16 homicides per 100,000 residents by 2014 placing Philadelphia as the sixth-highest city in the country.

The number of shootings in the city has declined significantly since the early years of the 21st century.

Shooting incidents peaked at 1,857 in 2006 before declining nearly 44 percent to 1,047 shootings in 2014. Major crimes have decreased gradually since a peak in 2006 when 85,498 major crimes were reported.

The number of reported major crimes fell 11 percent in three years to 68,815 occurrences in 2014, which include homicide, rape, aggravated assault, and robbery, decreased 14 percent in three years to 15,771 occurrences in 2014.

Philadelphia was ranked as the 76th most dangerous city in a 2018 report based on FBI data from 2016 for the rate of violent crimes per 1,000 residents in American cities with 25,000 or more people.

The latest four years of reports indicate a steady reduction in violent crime as the city placed 67th in the 2017 report, 65th in 2016, and 54th in 2015.

In 2014, Philadelphia enacted in ordinance decriminalizing the possession of less than 30 grams of marijuana or 8 grams of hashish; the ordinance gave police officers the discretion to treat possession of these amounts as a civil infraction punishable by a $25 ticket, rather than a crime.

Philadelphia was at the time the largest city to decriminalize the possession of marijuana. From 2013 to 2018, marijuana arrests in the city dropped by more than 85%. The purchase or sale of marijuana remains a criminal offense in Philadelphia.

Add

Now that Charlie had enlightened Sarge on the Philly Police Department, which was quite crucial to their current investigation into the ‘crime way’ in “The City of Brotherly Love”, he said to Sarge.

“Sarge, once again try to listen to this important information about the excellent **Chad Bianco’s** RCSD department, as he is assisting us with support for our assignment here in Philly.”

^^^^^

RIVERSIDE COUNTY [RCSD] HISTORY:
Current and Past Sheriff’s:

- Chad Bianco 2019-current
- Stanley Sniff 2007–2019
- Bob Doyle 2003-2007
- Larry Smith 1994-2002

- Cois Byrd 1986-1994
- Bernard Clark 1963-1986
- Joe Rice 1952-1963
- Carl Rayburn 1931-1952
- Clemens Sweeters 1924-1931
- Sam Ryan 1923-1924
- Frank Wilson 1907-1923
- P.M. Coburn 1899-1907
- W.B. Johnson 1895-1899
- Fred Swope 1893-1895

The **Riverside County Sheriff's Department** (RCSD or RSD), also known as the Riverside Sheriff's Office (RSO), is a law enforcement agency in Riverside County, in the U.S. state of California.

Overseen by an elected sheriff-coroner, the outstanding, Chad Bianco, the department serves unincorporated areas of Riverside County as well as some of the incorporated cities in the county by contract (see contract city).

Seventeen of the county's 26 cities, with populations ranging from 4,958 to 193,365, contract with the department for police services.

The county hospital and one tribal community also contract with the department for proactive policing. Riverside County is home to 12 federally recognized Indian reservations.

Absent proactive policing and traffic enforcement, the department is responsible for enforcing criminal law on all Native American tribal land within the county.

This function is mandated by Public Law 280, enacted in 1953, which transferred the responsibility of criminal law enforcement on tribal land from the federal government to specified state governments including California. The department also operates the county's jail system.

In addition to performing law enforcement and corrections roles, the department performs the functions of the coroner's office and marshal's office.

In its coroner function, the department is responsible for recovering deceased persons within the county and conducting autopsies.

When California reorganized its judicial system in the early 21st century and eliminated state marshal's offices, the department assumed responsibility for state courts within the county, providing court security and service of warrants and court processes.

The department also provides services such as air support, special weapons teams for high risk critical incidents, forensics services and crime laboratories, homicide investigations, and academy training to smaller law enforcement agencies within the county and in surrounding counties.

History:

RCSD deputies in December 2014

Riverside County was created from portions of San Bernardino and San Diego Counties on May 9, 1893. In the early history of the county, the sheriff's office was a one-person operation.

As the county grew in population, so too did the department, eventually transforming into a modern full-service law enforcement agency.

The department made national headlines on May 9, 1980, when five men armed with shotguns, an assault rifle, handguns, and an improvised explosive device robbed the Norco branch of "Security Pacific Bank".

Since dubbed the "Norco shootout", deputies responding to the bank robbery call, armed only with their pistols, confronted the perpetrators outside the bank and a prolonged gun battle and subsequent vehicle pursuit ensued.

The aftermath of the incident left 33 patrol cars damaged or completely destroyed, one sheriff's helicopter shot down, three robbers imprisoned for life, two robber's dead, eight sheriff's deputies wounded, and one deputy killed in the line of duty.

Today the Riverside County Sheriff's Department is responsible for 7,303 square miles, spreading almost 200 miles in length, and embracing approximately 50 miles in width. This territory constitutes the third largest county in the state of California and is roughly the size of the state of New Jersey in total area.

Vast changes have occurred in Riverside County since its incep-tion. The population, having increased from 13,745 in 1893, to more than 2,189,641 in 2010, ranks it fourth in population among California's counties behind Los Angeles, Orange, and San Diego Counties respectively. Expanding to keep up with the county's explosive growth, the Riverside County Sheriff's Department is now the second-largest sheriff's department and third largest police agency in California, with a staff of over 4,500.

County jail system:

The Riverside County Sheriff's Department operates the county's jail system. The Riverside County jails provide short-term and long-term (depending on the type of sentencing) incarceration services for the county, jailing subjects arrested and charged with various types of crimes pending their court disposition as well as those convicted of crimes and sentenced.

Services also include transportation of prisoners if necessary related to court appearances, and transferring prisoners between jurisdictions such as other counties, states, or the California Department of Corrections and Rehabilitation. Jails are staffed by fully sworn deputy sheriffs as well as specialized correctional deputies.

The county's jail system consists of the 'Robert Presley' Detention Center (RPDC) in downtown Riverside, the Southwest Detention Center (SWDC) in French Valley near Murrieta, the 'Larry Smith' Correctional Facility (SCF) in Banning, the Indio Jail, and the Blythe Jail.

The Riverside County Jail (RCJ) was renamed RPDC in 1989 with the completion of a new, modern jail facility across the street from the original jail.

The "Old Jail" was originally constructed in 1933 and was built as part of the old historic courthouse annex. In 1963, an addi-tion was made to the jail, which included dormitory style houses on all Native American tribal land within the county.

This function is mandated by Public Law 280, enacted in 1953, which transferred the responsibility of criminal law enforcement on tribal land from the federal government to specified state governments including California. The department also operates the county's jail system.

In addition to performing law enforcement and corrections roles, the department performs the functions of the coroner's office and marshal's office. In its coroner function, the department is responsible for recovering deceased persons within the county and conducting autopsies.

When California reorganized its judicial system in the early 21st century and eliminated state marshal's offices, the department assumed responsibility.

ACADEMY:

The Riverside Sheriff's Academy is located at the Ben Clark Public Safety Training Center (BCTC) near the March Air Reserve Base. Sheriff's academy training at BCTC is standardized and certified by the California Commission on Peace Officer Standards and Training (POST).

Trainees receive a minimum of 24 weeks of intensive training. The county's municipal police departments as well as other regional law enforcement agencies utilize the department's academy to train their cadets/trainees as well.

Upon successful completion of the academy, graduating Riverside County Deputy Sheriff Trainees also receive additional detention-specific training at the academy if they will be going to a jail posting for their first assignment (regardless of first assignment, all Sheriff's Deputies must eventually go to patrol if they wish to advance in rank/special assignment).

BCTC is also the location of the sheriff's corrections and dispatch academies. In addition, BCTC provides ongoing advanced career training for the department and surrounding agencies.

BCTC is a public safety training center jointly operated by the Riverside County Sheriff's Department and the Riverside County Fire Department in cooperation with the California Department of Forestry and Fire Protection, the California State Fire Marshal, the California Highway Patrol, and Riverside Community College.

Sheriff **Chad Bianco**, Riverside County Sheriff's Department, asked, "Charlie, how come you and Sarge get along so well during your very risky criminal and 'white collar' criminal invitations?"

Charlie thought for a moment, or two, and then replied, "Well, Sheriff, I really do not know. Even though he loves giving me a bad, very bad time, and also loves to call me old and senile, I know that he always has my-back and he would give is life for me in a heart-beat."

Sheriff, back to Charlie, "I think I understand now. He is like the brother that you never had but always wanted. And also like your right hand and personal body guard, right, Charlie?"

Then the Sheriff added before Charlie could reply, "Also, I think that Sarge is you alter-ego as well as your anti-hero, as well as he is slightly-flawed just like you. Well actually, if I may say so, Charlie you are more than 'slightly' flawed."

After which Chad laughed at the funny joke that he just made, and then laughed some more. Charlie, "Funny Sheriff, very funny. You are almost as clever as Sarge, but you misted the mark by a long way. But don't give up, you are getting better at your sense of humor."

Charlie jumps in now with, "No, Sheriff know it all, I am his personal body-guard not the other way around. I am so strong and tough that I really do not need him, I just keep him around because he makes me laugh."

And Charlie added, "You get it now Sheriff? You are getting as slow as Sarge, that is what happens when people hang around with him, they get old and slow. Look at what happened to me. I used to be quite fast and intelligent, and look at me now."

Sheriff Chad, not to be out done, comments, "But Charlie I would say that he is more correct than you are, so sorry to say. You seem to need him a lot, a whole lot, more than he needs *you*."

Charlie shot back not to be undone, "Wrong again, my little Sheriff friend. I keep telling you, and you do not seem to get it, slow on the up take are we Sheriff? I am the Alpha dog and Sarge is the Omega dog."

Charlie continues, "I bark louder than he does and I also scare criminals more than he does too." Sheriff, "Alright, alright Charlie, now let me see if I have this straight in my little, as you call it, mind."

Sheriff, "I just want to be clear on 'your' perception of your quasi-adversarial relationship with good old Sarge. You are the leader of the pack, so to speak, and he is just a follower, right?"

Charlie responds, very quickly, "Yes, see Sheriff you finally got it, albeit it took you long enough. But please do not tell him I said that, or else he will get a big head, and his head is already way, way big enough."

More *subterfuge* from our man Charlie, "Also Sheriff, he is my BFF (best friend forever), he really is and please do not tell him that I said that either, alright?"

CHAPTER EIGHT

CHARLIE KNOWS A GREAT deal about the LAPD (Los Angeles Police Department). He worked for them for many years as a Detective Lieutenant in the 'Robbery *and* Homicide' Division in Hollywood, and since that time, he has worked with them on several very high profile *'White Collar'* crimes in and around the 'City of *Angels'* (Los Angeles), California.

He is not that familiar, however, with the OCSD (*Orange County Sheriff's Department*), therefore he decided to do some background research on the great department since they were the *Lead* Agency in his subject case of the *theft* of the rare and quite valuable (or even priceless, perhaps) oil paintings by the 'Great Masters.'

Ray, the excellent and very experienced Chief of the outstanding *Laguna Woods Security* Department (the Private Security company that monitors and keeps LWV safe), used to be a Commander with the Orange County Sheriff's Department. And, prior to that, he was a State Trooper for 30 years for the New Jersey 'Staties' (New Jersey's Highway Patrol).

Charlie discovered very important background information while doing his normal due diligence and complete research of the OCSD and the private LWV Security Department. He wanted to know all about both of these departments as well as all of the key officers in each one.

Both agencies will be of great assistance to Charlie and his A-Team (all he needs now is Mr. T, remember the great old TV Show the *A-Team* with George Peppard and Mr. T) in solving this vile crime.

And his ever present (omnipresent) spirit of *survival*; shall guide him with this dangerous investigation as well, of course.

Orange County Sheriff's Department History:

The history of Orange County goes back further than the past *100* years and is a tribute to the adventurous spirit, personal drive, and tremendous courage of the early explorers and settlers whose vision and fortitude made cities where there were only dreams.

In any society, there are always challenges, but the pioneer men and women who forged Orange County out of a barren land had the courage to overcome the obstacles that stood in their path.

It wasn't until California became a state in 1850 that formal law enforcement institutions, based on the common law of England, became established. Even then, Southern California was a lawless society until the 1870s, plagued by rustlers, highwaymen, murderers, robbers, and swindlers.

Many made their headquarters in Los Angeles, blatantly defying the law and its traditional keepers-sheriff, jailor, judge and jury. Impromptu, poorly organized vigilante groups supplemented formal law enforcement officials, often taking the law into their own hands, but even these groups were ineffective.

The growth of communities, the increase in the number and proximity of small farms, and the improvement of both education and communication systems finally brought lawlessness under control.

Each formal community had its marshal, its constable, and its judge and when Orange County was formed in 1889, its citizens had a Sheriff directly responsible to them, and a new set of institutions right in their own backyard.

The Orange County Sheriff's Department today is a highly professional organization, which not only continues in its traditional role of crime suppression, but also has expanded into the area of crime prevention.

At the Orange County Sheriff's Department, you can see the spirit of adventure and the same courage as the early settler had. Orange County (as well as **Laguna Woods Village**) is a place where dreams have become a reality.

Orange County Sheriff's Department (California):

Formed: March 11, 1889

Size_948 square miles (2,460 km2)

Population:3,010,759

Deputies: 1460

Civilian: 1446

Agency executive: Sheriff

Jails: 4

Helicopters: 5

^^^^^

The Orange County Sheriff's Department is the law enforcement agency serving Orange County, California. It currently serves the unincorporated areas of Orange County and thirteen contract cities in the county:

Also, Aliso Viejo, Dana Point, Laguna Hills, Laguna Niguel, Laguna Woods, Lake Forest, Mission Viejo, Rancho Santa

Margarita, San Clemente, San Juan Capistrano, Stanton, Villa Park, and Yorba Linda, California.

The agency also provides law enforcement services to the Orange County Transportation Authority (OCTA) system and the John Wayne Regional Airport.

OCSD also runs Orange County's Harbor Patrol, which provides law enforcement, marine fire-fighting, search and rescue, and underwater search and recovery services along the county's 42 miles (68 km) of coastline and in the county's three harbors (Dana Point, Newport, and Huntington).

History OCSD:

J. Elliott, Joe Ryan, Sheriff Sam Jernigan, and Undersheriff Ed McClellan shown dumping bootleg liquor, circa 1925.

Early years:

The Orange County Sheriff's Department came into existence on August 1, **1889**, when a proclamation of the state legislature separated the southern portion of Los Angeles County and created Orange County.

The entire department consisted of Sheriff Richard Harris and Deputy James Buckley. They had an operating budget of $1,200 a year and a makeshift jail in the rented basement of a store in Santa Ana. They served a sparsely populated county of 13,000 residents scattered throughout isolated townships and settlements.

The problems faced by the first sheriff were typical for a frontier county–tracking down *outlaws*, controlling vagrancy, and attempting to maintain law and order across 782 square miles (2,030 km^2) of farmland and undeveloped territory.

But the county was expanding, and the department grew with it. The Spurgeon Square Jail was opened by Sheriff Joe Nichols in 1897 and the Orange County Courthouse followed in 1901.

Sheriff Theo Lacy (the second and fourth sheriff of Orange County, who served from 1890-1894 and 1899-1911) was able to move from borrowed office space in Santa Ana to a dedicated headquarters in the courthouse that remained in operation until 1924.

When he took office in 1911, Sheriff Charles *Ruddock* commanded a staff of eight full-time deputies and jailers, serving a county of nearly 34,000 citizens.

But the county's frontier past returned to haunt it on December 16, 1912, when Undersheriff Robert Squires became the first member of the department to be killed in the line of duty while he was part of a posse attempting to apprehend a violent fugitive.

The county's growing population brought new challenges. Most of the county had outlawed liquor by the time Sheriff Calvin Jackson took office in 1915. Raids of "blind pig" businesses that served as fronts for illegal liquor sales were commonplace. When Congress passed the 18th Amendment in 1920,

Prohibition became the law of the land. Suppressing illegal liquor operations became a major focus for the department over the next decade. By the time Sheriff Sam Jernigan took office in 1923, rum runners and bootleggers were commonplace along the coastline and in Orange County's harbors, using them as a base of operation for smuggling Canadian liquor into the country.

Thanks to Jernigan's diligence, many of them ended up serving time in the new county jail on Sycamore Street in Santa Ana, a building that would serve as OCSD's main jail and headquarters for the next forty-four years. Jernigan remained in office until the end of the decade.

By 1930 the department had grown to include eighteen full-time personnel with an operating budget of $49,582. The county's population was approaching 119,000, over half of which was scattered across a mostly rural landscape.

Sheriff Logan Jackson assumed office in 1931, and for the next eight years guided the department through a turbulent decade. The 'Long Beach' earthquake of 1933 caused widespread damage throughout the county, especially in Santa Ana.

In 1938, a week of intense rain overflowed the Santa Ana River, causing a massive flood that caused over $30 million in damage. The sheriff also had to deal with the Citrus Riots of 1936.

An agricultural labor dispute that led to a strike and subsequent disturbance so large that Sheriff Jackson swore in over four hundred special deputies to help control the violence.

But Jackson's term in office also saw advancements for the department, such as an expansion of the Sycamore Jail that included the county's first radio dispatch center. One of his final acts as sheriff was to implement the wearing of uniforms and a standardized badge for all thirty of his deputies.

Creation of the Reserve Bureau:

Sheriff Jesse Elliott replaced Jackson in 1939, just as the Depression was ending and the county once again began to prosper. This peaceful time was cut short by the outbreak of World War II in 1941, which created challenges unlike any others in department history.

Most of Orange County's peace officers left for war, leaving the department critically understaffed. This was made worse by the fact that in addition to his normal responsibilities, the sheriff was now required to assist with mandatory civil defense measures, such as air raid drills and blackouts, as well as help police the seven wartime military bases within the county borders.

Elliott suddenly found himself responsible for twice as many duties with only a fraction of his former staff to carry them out. To meet this need, he formed the Sheriff's Emergency Reserve, which eventually became the department's current Reserve Bureau.

^^^^^

CHARLIE OUR FAVORITE Private Investigator, only one of a few honest ones in the nation and the whole wide world, wanted to know a little bit more about the great OCSD (Orange County Sheriff's Department). He feels that knowing more about them, since they are the 'backbone' of Law Enforcement for all of Orange County, California, is crucial to his criminal investigation of a 'shooting in Laguna Woods'.

That way he would be better able to utilize all of their various departments and sections. He also would be able to pray for them as a whole as well as individually, for the good officers that he is working with to solve this heinous shooting case.

Then all of a sudden, Charlie, turned and said to Sarge, "My best amigo, before we look at more Orange County Sheriff's Department (OCSD) history, I just had a little *epiphany* and I want to share it with you."

And continued by saying, "They are coming for me, just like they did for 'Porter' and 'Parker' and our Lord and Savior, 'Jesus'. And, I shall meet them on the 'field of Battle', with my loyal and trusted, Sarge."

"And with Abba, out in front of us, we shall go amongst them and defeat our Archenemies at their own game, just like they were nothing."

Then Charlie added, "We shall not fret, we shall not *worry* and we shall not show any *fear* of them nor what they can do to our human bodies!"

"With help from our Dios, we shall *prevail*, we shall be *victorious*, we shall *defeat* them to their last warrior, and then we shall be *vindicated*."

After that, Charlie tacked on, "Sarge, you need to read and memorize more thoughts and ideas from the Book I told you about, remember?"

Now, it was Charlie's turn and he said, "Sarge lets back to the research on the history of the OCSD."

Post-World War II:

In 1946, retired NFL star and former deputy James A. Musick came home from the war and successfully ran for the office of sheriff, assuming command in 1947. He would serve as sheriff for the next twenty-eight years–the longest term in department history.

When he took office, the county was still mostly rural, with a population of 216,000 served by a department of only seventy-six. During Musick's administration, a number of divisions and facilities were commissioned that remain active to this day.

He implemented the county's first crime lab, its first Peace Officer's Training Center (now known as the Katella Facility), and the nation's first law enforcement Explorer post.

The 1960s saw the construction of the Orange County Industrial Farm (later renamed the James A. Musick Jail Facility), the Theo Lacy Facility, and the headquarters and central jails still in use today.

In response to the civil unrest of the late 1960s, Musick formed the Emergency Action Group Law Enforcement (EAGLE) team, a group of deputies with specialized training in various riot control and specialized tactics.

Although the team disbanded several years later, certain platoons evolved into the modern-day SWAT, Hazardous Devices, and Mounted Patrol units. The department grew even larger when the Coroner's Office merged with it in 1971.

By the time Musick retired in 1974, the county had expanded to a rapidly urbanizing population of over 1,400,000, with the department having grown to a staff of over 900.

Musick's handpicked successor was *Brad Gates*, who became sheriff in 1975. The department continued its rapid expansion during his administration, with the merging of two more agencies, the Orange County Harbor Patrol and the Stanton Police Department.

In response to severe jail overcrowding, the Intake Release Center was opened in 1988, completing the modern-day Central Jails Complex.

Gates also established the Air Support Bureau and created the Laser Village tactical training center, as well as the county's first DNA laboratory. The continuing urbanization of the county resulted in several cities incorporating and becoming contract patrol areas.

Gates also steered the department through the challenges of a severe county bankruptcy in 1994. By the time he retired in 1999, the department had grown to over 3,000 members.

Sheriff Carona:

Sheriff Michael Carona took office in 1999 and oversaw a merger of the Orange County Marshal's Department (his former agency) with OCSD. His term brought additional department expansion, including a modernized Katella Facility and a new OCSD Academy in Tustin.

Patrol cars were equipped with mobile computers, and anti-terrorism units were formed in response to the events of September 11, 2001. Carona received an initial surge in popularity due to the department's handling of high-profile cases such as the Samantha Runnion abduction and murder.

In 2007, Carona and a few of the former members of his executive staff were replaced. The county wanted some new blood, so to speak, in the quite large and complicated to manage, OCSD.

Carona's replacement, retired L.A. Sheriff's Commander *Sandra Hutchens*, was appointed by the county Board of Supervisors after a nationwide search for a suitable candidate.

Hutchens reorganized the agency after assuming office and created new branches such as the Homeland Security Division, a unified command for the various bureaus responsible for the county's security.

Subsequent economic challenges required large cuts to the department's budget and made it necessary to streamline the entire agency. Like a lot of big organizations Channel Design (Downsizing and/or *Mitigating*) is quite difficult to do, however, Sheriff Hutchens *and* her Executive Staff did a superb job.

^^^^^

Beds for Feds:

In 2010 OCSD and Immigration and Customs Enforcement (ICE) reached an agreement that would allow federal detainees to be placed in Orange County Jail facilities. Several deputies have been cross trained as ICE Special Agents.

Organization:

The OCSD is divided into twenty divisions covering five organizational functions: Public Protection; Jail Operations; Technical Services such as investigations, coroner services, emergency management; and Administrative and Support Services.

The Orange County Marshal's Department was absorbed by OCSD on July 1, 2000, then-Sheriff Michael Carona was the last Marshal. OCSD, under its Court Operations Division, now provides all security and law enforcement services (such as Bailiff services, weapons screening checkpoints, and prisoner custody) to the county court system.

The OCSD currently has 1,460 sworn deputies and over 1,446 civilian personnel, with another 800 reserve personnel.

Command Staff:

Executive Command:
Sheriff-Coroner, Undersheriff, Community Services, OC Crime Lab, and Public Affairs.
Administrative Services Command:
Executive Director and Senior Director
Communications and Technology
Financial/Administrative Services
Research and Development
Support Services

Custody Operations Command:

Assistant Sheriff, Commander, Central Jail Complex, Musick Facility, Theo Lacy Facility, and Inmate Services

Professional Services Command:
Assistant Sheriff, Commander, Court Services Bureau, Professional Standards, S.A.F.E., and Training Force

Field Operations and Investigative Services Command:
Assistant Sheriff, Commander, Coroner Medico Legal Investigations, and Airport Operations

Homeland Security, Investigations, North Operations, South Operations, Stanton Police Services, San Clemente Police Services, and OCTA Police Services

Charlie needed to take a break from his investigation into the OCSD. He had to make an encrypted cell Phone call to the FBI office in LA.

CHAPTER NINE

CHARLIE, OUR VERY famous or *infamous* some people would say, Detective now continues his information gathering into the excellent OCSD (*Orange County Sheriff's Department*). He found a lot of info on the great 'Agency' and he felt that it may come in handy with his investigation in, 'The City of Brotherly Love, Philadelphia' as well as his future criminal and 'white collar' cases in the OC, California later on.

He listed and emailed this important additional background (besides the information that he had already sent previously) to **Jan Smoker**, his outstanding cohort with his criminal investigations for the past five years, and also to the FBI, CIA, and also himself (to save on his office computer hard-drive, for future reference).

Sergeant Kevin Lybrand of the OCSD, Sarge and our man Charlie one day, were all standing around shooting the bull. Of course, according to Charlie, most of what Sarge said was B.S, and according to Sarge all of what Charlie says was B.S!

Sarge said to both of them, “I have to use the head, be right back, and please do not talk about me, Charlie, behind my back like you usually do, alright, Jefe?”

Charlie said to Kevin, “I think that I am going to tell good *Jason Danks*, the OCSD Captain in charge of the very needed and prestigious, ‘Community Policing department,’ that Sarge needs a refresher course at the outstanding OCSD Training Academy.”

Then he added to his sarcastic comment, “I am going to tell the Cap that Sarge is getting a little over weight, little slow on the draw of his gun, and putting on a little too much weight too.”

Charlie, “And I am also going to tell him that you are doing a great job helping my niño, Sarge, and the rest of our excellent A-Team, to help solve the ‘crime-wave’ in the ‘City of Brotherly Love, Philadelphia.”

He continued, just like he always continues, on and on and on, “Also, my good man, Kevin, you pick up things fast and you want to be the ‘first man’ through the door when we kick one in.”

And, “Just be sure that you do not to pick up any of Sarges bad habits, like talking too much. And telling jokes (about me), that are not funny, and stuff like that. Do you get my drift, Kevin?”

Charlie finally, finally, took a breath, and gave Kevin a chance to speak his piece, “Thank you very much Charlie, I appreciate the kind compliments and I can use them to ask Captain Danks for a big raise when I get back to Orange County."

Then he added, "And I know what you mean about Sarge, he is great guy, and I love him like a brother, but he is a little bit of a *whiner*. Also, he thinks that he is such a great Latin lover, but I do really do not know why?"

Charlie cut him off, because he likes to talk more than listen, "Kevin my new BFF, you have to understand how Sarge's *little* mind works. In it, that small thing/organ inside of his big head, he is a legend in his *own* mind, a real lady's man, with cat like reflects in a gun and/or knife fight."

Continuing his *diatribe*, Charlie says, "Now, Kevin, please do not ever, ever, tell Sarge that I said this, alright? But he actually is very well liked by the pretty *senoritas*, and he is the best man in the whole wide 'world' to have at your back during a shootout and sneak attack by the gangstas, the terrorists, and the other assundry bad guys, he truly is."

And on and on, "Also, Kevin, my man, I have seen Sarge go up against five or more gang-bangers without even hesitating. He is fearless, he really is. Now, that is something that you should copy from him, but not the bad jokes about me, OK?"

Kevin, spoke fast because he knew he would not have long before ole Charlie started up again, "Charlie, I agree with you. I have seen Sarge in very dangerous situations and he never, ever, backs down, to nobody."

Then he added, again very quickly, "Also, Charlie I have seen his other side how patient and kind he can be with children and women who come to the OCSD department and need help and assistance of one kind or another. He is very sympatric and understanding with each and every one of them, he really is."

Charlie cut in after he got his second wind, "Kevin, you are even sharper and observant than I thought that you were. You are absolutely correct, for I myself, have seen that softer and more gentle side of Sarge, when it is needed."

And, "I agree with you totally, he is excellent in every way, he truly is, but, but I repeat, which as you already I do a lot, never, ever, tell him that I said that, OK Kevin?"

Now Charlie said to both men, Sarge had gone to the head so therefore he had not heard their comments about him, "Here is some more information about the great OCSD and their Sworn and non-sworn officers."

Sworn:
Sheriff-Coroner (1)
Undersheriff (1)
Assistant Sheriff (4)
Commander (3)

Captain (12) / Chief Deputy Coroner
Lieutenant / Assistant Chief Deputy Coroner
Sergeant / Supervising Deputy Coroner
Investigator
Deputy Sheriff II / Senior Deputy Coroner
Deputy Sheriff I / Deputy Coroner
Reserve Deputy Sheriff

Non-sworn:
Sheriff's Special Officer III
Sheriff's Special Officer II
Sheriff's Special Officer I
Sheriff's Crime Scene Investigators
Sheriff's Correctional Services Assistant
Sheriff's Community Services Officer
Sheriff's Correctional Services Technician
Sheriff's Crime Prevention Specialists
Sheriff's Professional Staff
Sheriff's Cadets

Sheriff's Explorers: Explorer Commander (1):
Explorer Captain (4)
Explorer Lieutenant
Explorer Sergeant
Explorer Corporal
Explorer
Probationary Explorer

Facilities and Equipment:

Field and Investigative Services Command.

Homeland Security Division:

The division is composed of five separate bureaus, each with a nexus to local homeland security. Each one is run by a lieutenant or administrative manager. These bureaus are led by a Captain.

Special Enforcement Bureau (SWAT section/Air-Support Unit/Hazardous Devices Unit/Tactical Arrest Team/Crisis Negotiators Team).

Mass Transit Bureau (OCTA /Explosive Detection Unit/Module-Rail section).

Marine Operations Bureau (Newport Beach Station/Dana Point Station/Sunset-Huntington Station).

Mutual-Aid Bureau (Counter Terrorism section-JTTF/Grants/Sheriff's Response Team).

Orange County Intelligence and Assessment Center.

North Operations:

North Operations includes patrol and investigative services for the northern boundaries of Orange County. This division is based out of Sheriff's Headquarters in Santa Ana, California.

Villa Park, California

Rossmoor, California

Midway City, California

Orange Park Acres, California

Silverado Canyon, California

Modjeska Canyon, California

Yorba Linda, California

Unincorporated Anaheim, California

Unincorporated North Orange County

Emerald Bay, California

Stanton Police Services:

Stanton Police Services includes patrol and investigative services for the city of Stanton, California after the Stanton Police Department was absorbed by OCSD. The current head of Stanton Police Services is a Lieutenant.

Stanton, California

South Operations:

South Operations includes patrol and investigative services for the southern boundaries of Orange County. In 2015, South Operations was bifurcated into Southeast Operations and Southwest Operations. Southwest Operations is based in Aliso Viejo and led by a Captain.

Southwest Ops consists of the city's south and west of the I-5 freeway, Aliso Viejo, Laguna Hills, Laguna Woods, Laguna Niguel, San Juan Capistrano, Dana Point, and San Clemente.

Southeast Operations is based in Lake Forest and led by a Captain. Southeast Ops consists of the city's north and east off of the I-5 (Santa Ana) freeway.

Lake Forest, Mission Viejo, and Rancho Santa Margarita. Southeast Ops also houses the South Patrol Bureau, led by a Lieutenant. South Patrol Bureau provides general law enforcement services to the unincorporated communities of Wagon Wheel, Coto De Caza, Dove Canyon, Trabuco Canyon, Las Flores, Ladera Ranch, and Rancho Mission Viejo.

^^^^^

Aliso Viejo, California

Dana Point, California

Laguna Hills, California

Laguna Niguel, California

Laguna Woods, California

Lake Forest, California

Mission Viejo, California

Rancho Santa Margarita, California

San Juan Capistrano, California

Coto de Caza, California

Las Flores, California

Ladera Ranch, California

Wagon Wheel, California

Trabuco Canyon, California

Ortega Highway, California

San Clemente Police Services:

San Clemente Police Services includes patrol and investigations for the city of San Clemente, California. In 1992 San

Clemente Police Department was absorbed into OCSD, however San Clemente only allows the former San Clemente Police Station to be used by deputies who patrol their city. The current head of San Clemente Police Services is a Lieutenant.

Orange County Harbor Patrol - Marine Operations:

Orange County Harbor Patrol includes maritime security and enforcement of laws in Orange County's Harbors. Sheriff's personnel frequently work in conjunction with Federal Homeland Security and United States Coast Guard for interdiction of contraband and human trafficking. The current head of Harbor Patrol is Orange County Harbormaster, a Lieutenant.

Sunset Beach Harbor, California
Newport Harbor, California
Dana Point Harbor, California

John Wayne Airport Police Services:

John Wayne Airport Police Services provides responsive and professional service to John Wayne Airport. The Bureau consists of Deputy Sheriffs and Sheriff's Special Officers along with Explosive Detection Teams.

They pro-actively protect lives and property at this facility and respond to all calls for service promptly. In addition to these services they remain vigilant against threats (foreign or domestic) to ensure the security and safe operation of this facility.

All Airport Police Services employees are expected to represent the department and John Wayne Airport in a friendly, helpful, and professional manner. The current head of John Wayne Airport Police Services is a Captain.

OC Transit Police Services:

The mission of the OCTA Transit Police Services is to maintain a safe and peaceful environment for OCTA customers and employees, and to ensure the security of OCTA property. The current head of OCTA Police Services is a Lieutenant.

Training Division:

The Training Division develops, schedules, and presents law enforcement training for sworn peace officers and professional staff. The department utilizes two training sites ensuring the best learning environment possible, depending on the specific needs of the course.

Advanced officer training is primarily conducted at the Katella Facility in Orange. Academy and entry level training is primarily conducted at the Sheriff's Regional Training Academy in Tustin.

The Orange County Sheriff’s Department, as well as multiple local, state, and even federal public safety agencies, train at and utilize both sites.

Extensive input from law enforcement and other leaders throughout the county help to mold the curriculum and training that is offered. Both facilities are often utilized seven days per week and include daytime and evening instruction. The Division is led by a Captain.

The Orange County Sheriff's Regional Training Academy is located in Tustin, California on the site of the former Tustin Marine Corps Air Station. The facility opened in late 2007 and replaced the old academy on Salinas Avenue in Garden Grove which was no longer adequate due to overcrowding.

The Orange County Sheriff's Regional ‘Training Academy’ produces highly trained and professional Deputy Sheriffs & Police Officers, Sheriff's Special Officers, and Correctional Services Assistants. Some training is also conducted at a Sheriff's facility on Katella Avenue in the city of Orange, California.

The ‘Katella Training Facility’ in Orange, California houses the qualifications range, tactical range, administrative offices, advanced officer training, and elements of Homeland Security Division's Special Enforcement Bureau.

Some of the Orange County municipal agencies that send their recruit officers to OCSA include Newport Beach Police Department, Laguna Beach Police Department, Irvine Police Department, Costa Mesa Police Department, and University of California Irvine Police Department.

And also, the Fullerton Police Department, Garden Grove Police Department, Westminster Police Department, La Habra Police Department, Brea Police Department, Placentia Police Department, Tustin Police Department, and Orange Police Department.

Orange County residents are not the only recipients of the Orange County Sheriff's Academy's highly trained peace officers. Many Los Angeles County municipal police agencies send their recruits to be trained by the best at OCSA. Some of these agencies include;

Beverly Hills Police Department, Santa Monica Police Department, University of California Los Angeles Police Department, Torrance Police Department, Hawthorne Police Department, and Palos Verdes Estates Police Department.

And also, the Redondo Beach Police Department, Manhattan Beach Police Department, South Gate Police Department, Burbank Police Department, and Glendale Police Department.

Now on with the show.

The boys, Sarge, Kevin, and good ole Charlie, where chewing-the-fat again, when Sarge said to Charlie, "Tell me my senior citizen Jefe, exactly how old are you anyway?"

Charlie could not remember for sure, because he always says that he is younger than he really is (little white lies, he calls them), and then after a while replied, "Why do you ask my little 'jubbah Ut' niño?"

Sarge could not wait to tease his BFF, so he spit out, "I think that you must be the oldest PI (private investigator) in the world." "**What**!" Charlie practically yelled at Sarge.

When he had calmed himself down, at least a little bit anyway, he responded very slowly to the Sarges delight, "Sarge, little man, you might be right that I am getting a little bit older, but I can assure you that, I am still up to the task of putting the bad guys, and equally bad gals, behind bars, hopefully for a very, very long time."

Afterwards, Charlie continued his heavy breathing, he spoke, "And, if you do not believe me my niño, just ask the OCSD Sheriff, the OCDA, the RCSD, Chad Bianco, and *Captain Jason Danks*, and they will all tell you that I am still investigating, and having them arrest and prosecute lots, and lots of gang-bangers as well as terrorist's."

Sarge thought, and then immediately shot back at Charlie, "Perhaps my ole and well-respected *Jefe*, perhaps, but, but I repeat myself, you have to admit that you have slowed down at least a little bit on the up-take lately. And also, you are getting up there, I am sorry to tell you, my good old friend."

Sarge continued, as he could tell he was getting Charlie's goat and he absolutely loved when he was able to do that, "A significant slow-down Jefe, if I may once again repeat myself. A significant amount! And I am sorry that I am the one to have to tell you the bad news."

"Captain Danks, asked me just the other day, do you think that Charlie needs two OCSD-Sergeant's to cover his butt? Maybe even a LT (Lieutenant)?"

Charlie, now almost in full *cardiac arrest*, chocked, and came up off-of-the-ground about 6" and finally came back down and yelled, "Sarge, OK alright, yes, I do admit that I am getting older, but who is not, may I ask?"

Charlie Continued, "You by the way, my little son, are no *spring* chicken either, but I am still to young to hand up my guns and my polished hard-toe black police boots. You got that junior?"

Sarge smiled, he had a great smile and all of the ladies just loved it, and retorted, "OK, OK, my Jefe, I agree with you. You do have a few good years left in you, and furthermore, I want you to know, that I will be there to watch your back whenever you need me. I really will."

Now, Sarge's turn to continue, "Also, Charlie my old wise one and BFF, you can always count on me, and also Kevin Lybrand, as well as Captain *Danks* too."

Then it was Charlie's turn to smile, and he had a big smile on his face, he had a great smile also like Sarge, just ask him, "I always knew that you had my back, my niño and best partner ever."

Then he added, "OK, OK enough jabber, jabber lets go catch some bad guys you two, alright?"

CHAPTER TEN

THE LAST OF the quite important background about the OCSD that Charlie passed on to his 'A-Team' assisting him with the 'crime-wave' in "The City of Brotherly Love, Philadelphia," criminal case is listed herewith:

The **Sarge** has spent ten years with the great Orange County Sheriff Department and he added some facts about the great law enforcement organization to Charlie. Charlie knew more about the LAPD (Los Angeles Police Department) but Sarge knew more about the OCSD, naturally since he worked for them.

They often shared 'war-stories' about each- others favorite agency. While Charlie dearly loved the OCSD his heart and soul was still with the LAPD where he worked for 20 years. Here is what **Sarge** added to what he had already shared with Charlie about the OCSD.

Jails:

OC Central Jail Complex in Santa Ana, California.

The OCSD Custody Operations Division operates four (4) jails:

Central Men's Jail and Women's Jail - The Central Jail Complex, opened in 1968, is located next to the department offices in Santa Ana. It houses approximately 2,664 inmates. In January 2016, three inmates escaped from the jail.

Intake Release Center (IRC) - In 1988, as a part of the Central Jail Complex, the Intake Release Center was built to facilitate the intake and processing of inmates, and the including medical screening, booking, proper identification, and transfers between facilities.

While it is a transitional facility, it also holds male and female inmates for brief periods.

Theo Lacy Facility - The TLF, located in the city of Orange, was originally built in 1960. A major expansion, completed in 2006, brought its capacity to 3,100 inmates, making it the largest jail in the county.

James A. Musick Facility - A minimum security facility located on unincorporated county land near Lake Forest and Irvine, "The Farm" provides custodial and rehabilitative programs for 1,256 adult male and female inmates.

Courts:

After the Orange County Marshal's Department was absorbed by OCSD, the Sheriff's department became responsible for providing court services. There are Sheriff's personnel stationed at the Justice Centers throughout the County.

Sheriff's staff at the Justice Centers fulfill the vital mission of the Sheriff that include bailiff services in each courtroom and weapons screening operations in the lobby of each Justice Center. Each justice center houses a detention holding facility for inmates who are appearing in court each day.

These detention facilities are staffed by Deputy Sheriffs. There are also Deputies assigned to Civil Bureau who are out every day serving court documents, serving restraining orders, and conducting evictions.

The Special Operations and Judicial Protection Unit provides specialized protective and investigative services to counter any threats, perceived or real, towards the judiciary of the Superior Court of California, County of Orange.

All of these personnel fall under the Court Operations Command of the OCSD Professional Services Command. The current head of court operations is Captain Jim Rudy.

Orange County Sheriff's **Offices** are located at the following Superior Court of California facilities in the County of Orange:

Central Justice Center (CJC) in Santa Ana, CA

Lamoreaux Family & Juvenile Law Justice Center (LJC) in Orange, CA

North Justice Center (NJC) in Fullerton, CA

West Justice Center (WJC) in Westminster, CA

Harbor Justice Center (HJC) in Newport Beach, CA

Aircraft:

The department's 5 helicopters are (3 Euro copter AS350 B2 (or "A*Stars") and 2 rescue UH-1H Huey's) that use the radio call sign "Duke" (after actor and former Newport Beach resident John Wayne) and, appropriately, use John Wayne Airport as their operational base.

The original "Duke" helicopters (a pair of Boeing 500's) had an image of John Wayne riding atop a sheriff's badge (while waving his cowboy hat) painted on the fuselage.

The Aviation Unit covers the 13 contract cities the department serves, unincorporated communities, as well as a contract with the Santa Ana police department.

Orange County Sheriff's Department Explorer Post 449:

In November 1959, Orange County Sheriff James A. Musick wanted "young men," who desired exposure in the field of law enforcement to be afforded the opportunity to do so.

In a newspaper article he stated, "We organized the group after we found that other special interest Explorer Posts were taking our best young men from our high schools.

We decided, rather than take what was left over after other fields of endeavor took the best, that we should start training young men of high school age now for a career in law enforcement."

Thus, the first Law Enforcement Exploring Post in the nation was established. Its purposes were, "To train young men of today for the future that awaits them in the law enforcement field of tomorrow.

To stimulate young men's interest in law enforcement practices, the code of ethics, and the fine qualities of citizenship which are expected, to briefly explore all phases of law enforcement, and to be a definite approach to juvenile decency."

Post 449 began with twenty-eight explorers in Santa Ana who had to meet the qualifications of being between 14 and 21, must maintain a "B" average in school, have a clean record, be of outstanding citizenship in their community, and have a general reputation beyond reproach."

In 1973, after fifteen years of only young men being allowed in the Exploring program, Boy Scouts of America allowed young women to explore careers in law enforcement through membership in an Explorer Program. Maintaining the same high standards for qualification and training these young women diversified the Department's Post.

When the residents of contract cities and the unincorporated county area need help, they call the Sheriff's Department; when the Sheriff's Department needs help, they call on their Explorers.

The 'Orange County Sheriff's Explorer Post' supports deputies during road closures caused by natural disasters such as mud-slides, floods, and forest fires. They complete search missions where either missing persons or evidence is sought and are deployed to protect crime scene perimeters.

This involvement by the explorers allows Deputies to be available for calls for service. Explorers are also used to assist in public education. They distribute brochures explaining changes in parking regulations or temporary street closures.

During Bicycle Rodeo Events, Explorers demonstrate to children how to properly size and wear bicycle helmets. They offer child identification and crime awareness, through a "Kid-Print" program and assist in crime prevention demonstrations throughout the county.

^^^^^

The Department's Explorers serve the community by providing crowd and traffic control during Basic Academy Graduations, County Building Dedications, Mall grand openings, Community awareness fairs, 10 K runs, parades, and a multitude of other charitable events.

The Post's Color guard is used to present the flag at City Council and County Board of Supervisor meetings, as well as scouting and civic events.

The Orange County Sheriff's Department 'Explorers' participate in Law Enforcement competitions throughout the state. Through the use of the Department's "Laser Village" and its Training Staff, Post 449 Explorers have learned skills which enabled them to win several awards in Felony Car Stop. D.U.I., Bomb Threat and Search and Building Search scenarios. The Explorers also compete in Tug-of War, Volleyball and Obstacle Course competitions.

Sheriff's personnel, who volunteer as Advisors for the Department's Post, contribute countless hours exposing youths to Law Enforcement Careers. Their commitment to the advancement of the Exploring program goes beyond the Department's Post.

The Department's advisors also serve on the County-wide Organization as Ranking Officials, Academy Directors, Tactical Training Officers and Instructors at the Explorer Academy.

In addition to Orange County, these Advisors have trained and taught Explorers in Kern, Los Angeles, San Diego, Riverside, and Ventura counties.

List of the excellent, very devoted and outstanding former sheriffs:

Richard T. Harris (1889–1891)

Theo Lacy (1891–1895)

Joe C. Nichols (1895–1899)

Theo Lacy (1899–1911 = Second term)

Charles Ruddock (1911–1915)

Calvin E. Jackson (1915–1923)

Sam Jernigan (1923–1931)

Logan Jackson (1931–1939)

Jesse L. Elliott (1939–1947)

James A. Musick (1947–1975)

Brad Gates (1975–1999)

Michael Carona (1999–2008)

Jack Anderson (Assistant Acting Sheriff)

(January 2008 to June 2008)

Sandra Hutchens (2008–2018)

Don Barnes (2018 - present).

Charlie then told Sarge, "If you keep doing the outstanding job as a Sergeant at the OCSD (Community Citizen Protection and Policing Section) you will soon become a LT (Lieutenant), then a Captain, then a Commander, then the Undersheriff, and before you know it, one day, you will be the OCSD *Sheriff*."

Sarge stuttered, then finally replied, "Charlie, my favorite Hefa ever, I sincerely appreciate your confidence and support of my career, I really do, but, I do not feel that I will ever become any of those positions, ever."

Charlie laughed, and laughed again, "My trusted 'Tubbs' I cannot believe that you are being modest? You are always bragging about being the best deputy in the OC and now you say you are not qualified to be Sheriff."

Charlie then continued, "And by the way, you are the *best* Sergeant at the OCSD, even though there are also lots of excellent ones there as well besides yourself. Also, you have one of the most dedicated to serving the public and the honest tax paying and law -abiding citizens of the OC that I have ever seen."

Charlie said more, he was on a *roll*, you know old Charlie when he gets up on his 'soap-box', so to speak. "And I do not want you to get a big head, as yours is big enough I can assure you, just as your ego, but you have one of the best and most caring personalities of anyone in law enforcement that I know."

Finally, Sarge retorted, "Charlie my hero, then he laughed, ha, ha, I really appreciate all of your interest and support for my career, but I think that you are just a little bit biased because I have saved your life so many times."

Charlie shot back, "What are talking about? I am the one who has saved your 'bacon' many times, not the other way around. And besides, I was not trying to boast about you, I was telling the truth, You, are a great man, Sarge you truly are, so get over it, OK?"

Charlie felt like he now knew a tremendous additional amount about the great OCSD and their excellent current Sheriff (**Don Barnes**). After all of the above research and also talking to lots of people inside, as well as outside, of the department, he is very comfortable with letting them assist him with all of his criminal investigations in the OC (Orange Country, California).

The local Sheriff's Department Patrol site is located in Aliso Viejo, California, which is very close to the Laguna Woods Village. Their excellent Officer's patrol LWV 24/7, and *Charlie* noted their patrol cars several times while on the job at LWV.

Normally the *FBI* takes over control on a quite high-profile case such as this one because they want the National exposure (e.g. press and news coverage), however, *Charlie* insisted that the Philly Police Department with Sarge representing the *OCSD* could handle it with the limited assistance of the FBI and himself, of course.

CHAPTER ELEVEN

DOCTOR BRETT LONG (Charlie's terrific Chiropractor) called Charlie from Lake Forest, California out of the blue, and asked," Charlie, old-timer how is your bad back, your bad neck, your bad concussion, and your bad 'everything' doing?"

Charlie thought for a few moments, and then spoke slowly, he is doing everything slowly these days, after being shot and also sustaining a severe and 'permanent' brain concussion, "Hi Doc nice to hear from you, but what do you mean by old-timer?"

He continues, of course just like he always does, "I am as spry as a spring chicken. And by the way, I am still taller, better looking and smarter than you are." Not one to keep his big mouth shut, "And Bailey told me so."

Doc Long, "Yeah, right Charlie in your dreams, now you know that Bailey did *not* say that, and if you keep lying like that your big nose is going to get even bigger. You remember *'Pinocchio'* don't you?"

The doctor continues, "Yes, Bailey, thinks that you are a nice and funny guy, and she is not normally wrong about people she meets however, I am not quite sure why she thinks that *you* are funny, intelligent or nice?"

And more, "Maybe, just maybe you will be the first person that she was wrong about old-timer?'

Charlie could hardly control his laughter, and finally spit out his retort, "Doc, you are a great chiropractor, but you just do not know a superior being when you meet one, me for example."

Doctor was busy, as always and needed to get back to his other less demanding and less senile patients, "Enough levity for now old-timer, Bailey and I are catching the next 'Red Eye' (flight) out of the famous John Wayne (Orange County) Airport in Costa Mesa/Santa Ana, California."

Doc Long continued in a hurried voice, "Bailey said she thought that she could help with your criminal investigation in 'The City of Brotherly Love, Philadelphia,' and also that I need to make some needed adjustments and such to your old and worn-out body."

Then he added, "So she said we both needed to get to Philly, as soon as possible, to help that old, decrepit Private Investigator, Charlie. Alright, she did not call you decrepit, I was just funning you, ha-ha."

Charlie then says to Sarge, "I love it when things come together, don't you Sarge?" Sarge replies, "I know where you got that saying from Jefa, it comes from that great old TV show *'The A-Team'* with George Peppard and Mr. T, right?" Charlie thinks that Mr. T. is way, way cool. He saw him on *'Dancing with the* Stars' a few years ago.

And for a big, strong man, he still has some moves like the superstar 'Leon Patillo' lead vocalist and co-founder for the outstanding Rock group, '**Santana**.' Charlie thinks that Carlos Santana is one of the best-rockers ever, even though he does not get as much attention as the other rock 'n roll singers.

He then quickly added, "On our next investigation, I want to be Mr. T and you can be George, alright Charlie?" Charlie chuckled, and said, "Sure, my niño, whatever you want."

Charlie, Sarge and the rest of his incredible A-Team, determined that there were in reality three groups responsible for the horrific 'crime way' in "The City of Brotherly Love, Philadelphia."

1. Responsible for most of the *Jewelry* Heists, was the New 'Pink Panthers' gang. As it turned out, there were lots of druggy's that were stealing 'bling' so that they could pone them for money to buy drugs with.

However, the vast majority of jewelry story thefts were done by the extremely fast, and well-organized Pink Panther gang. They were in and out in less than three minutes, somehow, and no one would see them come or see them go!

2. Responsible for all of the Bank *Robberies* was the "Flaming Sword" gang from Nigeria. Sarge had told Charlie earlier that he though that there were several different bank robbers. It turned out, however, that because robbing a bank is a Federal Offense, not many crooks wanted to take that chance.

The 'Swords' were from out of the country, and were here illegally, smuggled into the United States right close to the *Tijuana*, Mexico border. Right where they are building the very needed border wall.

Charlie then said that the 'third' leg of the Philly 'crime wave' is as followers:

3. Responsible for *most*, but not all, of the '*Drive*-by' *Shootings*, was the savage and 'vitriolic' and notorious, 'MS-13 Gang.' Philly like most of the major cities in American is filled with 'want to be' gangsters, who on a regular basis have turf-wars and do drive shootings just because they do not work, have nothing else to do, and want more drug 'corners'.

These, young wana-be's, *hoodlums,* are referred to as *'Top Boys'* and they are not afraid of being shot, or stabbed, and or even killed by the OG's (original gangster's) or the MS-13.

EPILOGUE

JUST AS SOON as our man, and our favorite PI, Charlie got back from his very dangerous assignment in 'The City of Brotherly Love, Philadelphia', and before he could even unwind, he got an encrypted satellite cell phone call, *"From Russia with Love."*

A CIA (Central Intelligence Agency-in Langley, Virginia) double agent working in *Vladimir Putin's* Kremlin office in Moscow, Russia was just arrested by the FSB (formerly the hated KGB). The FSB has the same old faces as did the KGB, like **Vladimir Putin**, as just *one* example.

Putin then told former United States of America President Donald Trump, that he would exchange him for the recently arrested by the FBI, a quite lovely and very sexy *'Red Sparrow'* woman spy.

There was just out a great movie and a 'Red Sparrow' and most of the people who saw it did not realize that there are actually a number of these 'shady' lady spies in the USA today (and there have been since the old 'Cold War' days in the 1960's).

She operated and did her 'espionage' out of a luxurious penthouse suite in Washington, DC (at the famous or infamous, *Watergate* Tower), and 'cultivated' relationships with congress men and others in government to get secret and *classified* information for her handlers and the Russian government.

Charlie was doing more research and investigation on this little 'bird' (Red Sparrow). And he told Sarge, "see I told you that you could not trust those *'commie' pinko's*, remember?"

The Director of the CIA *Xavier Becerra* (Formerly the *'Attorney General'* for the great State of *California*) was on the other end of the encrypted cell phone, and he wanted Charlie and Sarge to go to the *Ukraine* (one of our allies) just across the border with Russia, and sneak across the border and rescue the double agent (Boris Alexander Sovenkyvic).

Charlie called Brett Long and Bailey, at their Lake Forest Private Detective Agency, for some information concerning people inside the Iron Curtain. It is had to find out anything that goes on inside Russia, just like it the old days, but now a little bit more Capitalistic.

Charlie told Sarge, "*Vladimir* **Putin**, Russia's infamous Premier/President, boasts about being the richest man in the whole world. He was the former head of the FSB (which is the old KGB with new name, but same old faces), and still pulls all of the strings

That means that you can buy almost anything, including intel if you have the right amount of money. Bailey negotiated a fair deal with Alexander 'Peter' *Nitscofranko* a top FSB Interrogation Officer who worked at the Kremlin.

Charlie told Sarge, "The Kremlin is a dark, dank, and sinister place. I have been there once while on an assignment for the CIA, but in the day. I still can feel the hairs on the back of my neck standing up while I was inside that vitriolic building.

Bailey knew a guy who knew a guy who worked for the FSB (Russian Secret Police), formerly the KGB. It is just like our CIA (Central Intelligence Agency) except more deadly, much more deadly.

She was able to get the information that Charlie and Sarge needed, in no time at all. Even the CIA could not find out what she did in that short amount of time. She was a terrific Private Eye, and very cute to boot.

Charlie then said to Sarge, "I have a feeling in the pit of my, stomach, in my gut, that my 'tour of duty' (my life so to speak), solving criminal investigations, and putting bad guys behind bars in the United States (and or in deep dank black ops prison in Europe), in this crazy ole mixed up world, is almost over my niño."

And then Sarge responded very quickly, to his loyal and trusty sidekick and BBF, "Charlie, this is *no time to Die'*, not yet anyway, as your hero James Bond, 007, always says."

Charlie had to add one more- little note, doesn't he always? "By the way Sarge, my man of little Movie knowledge, Sean Connery was the best 'James Bond' in the 007 Movies, out of all of the other men who portrayed Bond."

Charlie saw a recent photo of Connery the other day on the internet, he is almost 90 now, and looks kind of old and worn out just like Sarge says he does!

And then Sarge added, once again very fast, he talks faster than Charlie can think, he always says, "And always remember Charlie, 'keep you head on a swivel', and also watch your- back out there my old Hefa."

Then in a heart-beat, less than 60 seconds, our man Charlie the PI, was gone!

www.ingramcontent.com/pod-product-compliance
Lightning Source LLC
Chambersburg PA
CBHW030615310726
48979CB00003B/728
9781732628335